Dangerous Trespass

Madeline knew she had no business on the grounds of Balenger Hall. But they had been deserted for so long, and were so beautiful on a bright sunny day.

So she had trespassed—and was now paying the penalty.

The man who had appeared suddenly was clearly no gentleman. His sun-streaked hair, tanned face, the scar on his arm, his callused hands that now seemed ready to close upon her shoulders, spoke of a life a world away from that of good breeding and polite society—nor was the way this powerfully built, strikingly handsome stranger looked at her the way that any gentleman should or would.

Never, indeed, had she encountered any man who seemed less a gentleman—and who made her feel less a lady. . .

The
Secret Nabob

Martha Kirkland

A SIGNET BOOK

SIGNET
Published by the Penguin Group
Penguin Books USA Inc., 375 Hudson Street,
New York, New York 10014, U.S.A.
Penguin Books Ltd, 27 Wrights Lane,
London W8 5TZ, England
Penguin Books Australia Ltd, Ringwood,
Victoria, Australia
Penguin Books Canada Ltd, 10 Alcorn Avenue,
Toronto, Ontario, Canada M4V 3B2
Penguin Books (N.Z.) Ltd, 182–190 Wairau Road,
Auckland 10, New Zealand

Penguin Books Ltd, Registered Offices:
Harmondsworth, Middlesex, England

First published by Signet, an imprint of Dutton Signet,
a division of Penguin Books USA Inc.

First Printing, January, 1996
10 9 8 7 6 5 4 3 2 1

To the Cotters:
Adelaide, Ouida, Jacque, and Bill

To the Thompsons:
Jolie, Joshua, Daniel, and Juliet

and

To my dear friend:
Helena Carter Robisch

Chapter 1

"Blast, and double blast!" Madeline Wycliff muttered. "I am trapped."

Tossing her quill onto the ink-stained blotter of the scarred, cubbyhole desk, she got up from the straight-back chair and tiptoed to the heavy oak door, closing it just in time before her arguing relatives entered the parlor adjoining her hiding place. In hopes of finding privacy, Madeline had retired to the back of the house, to the little room that had in better times been the office of the house steward. In the past year this room had become her domain, the place where she did the household accounts and wrote letters for the basket weavers. On normal days, she would not have been disturbed.

But today was not normal.

Today her sister had arrived from London, unannounced and in an agitated state that spoke as plain as a pikestaff, *I need money.* And though Madeline would probably be taken roundly to task for absenting herself from the protracted welcome, she had no wish to witness her mother's joy at the visit of her middle daughter—the first visit home since Arabella's wedding trip. Madeline had even less desire to be in the company of her sister—the special pet of both parents—spoiled from infancy, and showing no signs of having abandoned her self-indulgent lifestyle since becoming Lady Townsend.

Unfortunately the chamber in which Madeline sat had only one door, and it opened into the parlor. She was truly caught.

"You always were selfish, Bella," Miss Priscilla Wycliff fairly shouted, "but *this* I would not have believed even of you. I credited you with at least a modicum of sisterly loyalty."

Mrs. Wycliff shushed her youngest daughter, a damsel only just turned seventeen, and bade her hold her tongue until she closed the parlor door. "For you know how the servants talk."

"It is as well they do," Priscilla replied, "for otherwise I would never have learned of Bella's duplicity. I still cannot believe that I alone knew nothing of the episode."

Madeline, an unwitting eavesdropper on this scene, found herself listening with a most unladylike degree of interest. Opening the door a crack, just enough to see the occupants of the parlor, she spied her middle sister.

As much as Madeline hated to admit it, Bella looked splendid, attired in one of the ensembles purchased as part of her bride's clothes, a trousseau whose debt still had not been discharged. The traveling costume, a jade green faille dress with a matching velvet spencer, complemented the twenty-two-year-old beauty's titian hair and warmed her hazel eyes; at the moment these eyes filled charmingly with tears—a talent improved upon over the years.

"I am not selfish," the beautiful Arabella informed the youngest of the three Wycliff sisters. "And as to your not knowing the facts of my come-out, you were but a child at the time."

"It was two years ago. I was fifteen, quite old enough to understand the story of one sister stealing what belonged to the other."

"Stealing! It was no such thing. Mama, tell her that it was for the good of the family."

Zoe Wycliff sat on a pale yellow brocaded sofa, her plump hand on her ample bosom, her pale lashes fluttering over green eyes. Though her still reddish hair was no longer the crowning glory it had been when she married Lewis Wycliff twenty-seven years ago, the matron's looks gave evidence of the beauty that was once hers—a beauty not unlike that of her favorite daughter, Arabella. "It was truly for the best."

Fumbling in her reticule for her smelling salts, should a well-timed swoon become necessary, she continued, "I had not thought to be able to send any of my daughters to town for the Season, what with your papa always being behindhand with the world. Then suddenly there was Mrs. Hazlip offering to take one of them along with her own shy little Sarah, and I had to make a choice."

"Not *one* of them, Mama," Priscilla argued. "Mrs. Hazlip invited Madeline. You know she wanted Maddy; Sarah and Bella were never friends." Unable to contain her outrage, the young girl flounced over to the casement window that offered a view of a side garden in need of a good scything, then plopped down on the window seat whose chintz cushions had long ago lost both their shape and their color. "But even if the Hazlips had not invited Maddy by name, she is the oldest daughter; she was entitled to the first come-out."

Priscilla's lake blue eyes flashed with anger. "It was Maddy's chance to meet eligible young men, for you know there are no gentlemen of suitable age in our district. Her one chance. And you took it, Bella! Somehow you convinced Papa that Maddy would be unable to secure a husband and that the opportunity should be given to you."

Arabella refused to admit culpability. "Have you forgotten that when the Hazlips went to London, Madeline was already three and twenty? *I* was but twenty at the time. Therefore, it was decided that I had a better chance of forming an alliance that would help restore the family finances."

Priscilla shook her head in disbelief, making her flaxen curls bounce. She looked about her at the shabby furniture, the threadbare carpet. "Well, then, sister, you are Lady Townsend now; when do you mean to start bestowing your husband's largesse upon us? If that was the purpose of your usurping the come-out, to snare some wealthy gentleman to whom we could all turn in time of trouble, where is he now? Please, I beg of you, do not waste another minute. Show us Mr. Plump Pockets."

"Priscilla!" her mother cautioned, "do not speak in that vulgar manner, or I shall be forced to send you to your room."

"I may be vulgar, Mama, but I have spoken only the facts. No point in wrapping the story in clean linen, for *we* at least know the truth."

"Really, Mama," Arabella said haughtily, "must I be subjected to such vilification on my first day home?"

"Of course not, my love. Priscilla, leave us at once. And I will thank you to speak no more upon this subject, for you know nothing of the situation."

"I know enough."

The young lady walked to the parlor door but paused just before her hand touched the knob. "And for your information, Bella, the truth is never vilification. You tricked Maddy out of her chance to meet an eligible *parti*. You know it and I know it. And what do you do? You marry to suit yourself, choosing a gamester whose only unencumbered assets are his dubious skill at cards and his handsome smile."

"Mama!" Arabella protested, "make her apol—"

"Out!" ordered her indignant parent. "No one wishes to listen to the rantings of a young, stupid gel."

In that statement, however, Mrs. Wycliff was wrong. One person, at least, heard the young lady's words with more than passing interest. Seated at her desk, her hands clasped tightly in her lap to still their trembling, Madeline had listened to her sister's sincere championing and experienced a moment of gratification. The past was the past, of course, and there was nothing to be gained by rehashing old grievances, but Madeline was human enough to admit she was pleased that at least one of her family saw the injustice of what had occurred.

Although, how her youngest sister had learned the story of the come-out that never was, she did not know. *She* had certainly never mentioned it. Eight years separated Madeline and Priscilla, and though she and the seventeen-year-old were very much attached to one another, they were not close enough for confidences of that nature, confidences that involved wounded pride and feelings of betrayal.

Realizing that Arabella was in the middle of an impassioned explanation of some kind, Madeline brought her thoughts back to the present.

"I tell you," vowed the new Lady Townsend, "I had no choice. I had to come home."

"You did just as you ought, my love, for where else should a woman turn but to the bosom of her family."

"To her husband's bosom!" Bella declared. After a bout of theatrical sniffs, she added, "Only Orville is gone."

"Gone! Surely you cannot mean . . ." Mrs. Wycliff pressed her hand to her chest. "My heart! My palpitations! You cannot mean that Townsend has deserted you."

"No, no," Bella answered, lowering the bit of lace and

lawn she'd held pressed to the corners of her eyes. "Not deserted, Mama, only gone away for a while. Just until these men who are threatening him—these *Greek banditti*—take themselves elsewhere."

Continuing her story, Bella said, "The mortgage is due next quarter day, and Townsend could think of no way to raise the money save gaming. And since that is the route by which he got into this predicament in the first instance, I could not persuade myself that his skill at cards would miraculously improve. I was in the right of it. Now these *banditti* want their money, and *I* cannot give it to them."

Mrs. Wycliff gasped. "Never tell me they approached you for it."

"They did. And a nastier set of rogues you never saw. Penburne told them Townsend was gone to the country, but when the old butler tried to shut the door, they pushed their way past him and came directly up the stairs to the small saloon where I sat. I quite feared for my life, for I had believed one of the men wore a pistol beneath his coat."

At this news her parent cried out, "Oh, my dear, dear child."

"That is the reason for my sudden flight, without so much as a note to warn you of my arrival. But you need not worry that I have come home to ask Papa for the money. I know better than that."

"Certainly you do, my love, for your father is forever in dun territory. Though I am persuaded that if he had any money, which, of course, he does not, he would happily expend some of it upon your dear husband."

Madeline lifted grateful eyes heavenward, relieved that neither woman was so foolish as to believe the estate could support another man whose pastimes exceeded his pocketbook. Money—or the lack thereof—was the catalyst for most of the Wycliff family crises. Wybourne, though not a large estate, was a productive one and provided the family with all the necessities and even a few of the niceties of life. It might possibly have provided them with a few luxuries as well, had it not been for Lewis Wycliff's love of sport and the expenses attending that pursuit.

"But if you do not borrow the money from your father, where will you get it?"

Arabella hesitated, as though searching for a way to broach a delicate subject. "Mama, did you ever meet old Balenger's heir?"

At the seeming non sequitur, Mrs. Wycliff stared blankly at her daughter. "I never met Horace Balenger himself above a half dozen times, never mind that our lands run side by side or that our homes are scarce two miles' distance apart, for he was a thoroughly disagreeable gentleman. I remember once he—"

"Not the old man, Mama. His heir. Did you ever meet him?"

"Do you mean his son?"

"No, I refer to his grandson. The son, Mr. Samuel Balenger, died several years ago in India. At any rate, that is what I heard had happened to him."

"Well, that is too bad, I am sure, but what have the Balengers to do with anything? Or the Balenger heir, for that matter. Not that it is of much use to be an heir when there is nothing left to inherit. Balenger Hall was once a handsome place, but the old martinet let it fall into shocking disrepair. It would require a fortune to bring the place around."

Arabella smiled, warming to the subject. "That is just the point, Mama. The grandson has a fortune. Pots and pots of it, according to the *on-dits*."

Mrs. Wycliff sighed dreamily. "Pots of money. What a

lovely sound that has. I am persuaded it must be deliciously comfortable to have all the money one needs. Though, I still fail to see—"

"Mama," interrupted her daughter, "the heir is a bachelor!"

Much struck by this interesting piece of information, Mrs. Wycliff's mouth fell open in a most ungenteel manner. "A bachelor. My love, are you certain?"

"Quite. Once the many parties and fetes celebrating our dear Princess Charlotte's marriage to Prince Leopold were at an end, all one heard discussed in town was Balenger. 'The nabob,' they call him. He has been there for the last few weeks, and as you can imagine, all the matchmaking mamas are pursuing him for their daughters. But it is rumored that he plans to leave London soon, to take up residence at the Hall."

"He is coming here? To Little Easton? Oh, my dear child, what wonderful news. A wealthy bachelor at the Hall. I cannot believe that destiny has finally smiled upon us. And me, with a daughter as yet unmarried." With a sigh of pure exultation, she added, "Oh, my fortunate, fortunate Priscilla."

Though the eavesdropper, still hidden behind the partially closed door, flinched as though her flesh had been pierced by some sharp barb, not so her sister; on Arabella's face was a look of satisfaction. "I see that we are of one mind, Mama. All the way down here I kept hoping, praying that my sister had grown into a presentable young lady. But the situation is even better than I had dreamed of, for she has become a real beauty. A diamond, in fact. And by a happy chance, fair ethereals are in fashion this year. Now I am certain my plan will work."

"Your plan?"

"Yes. A plan whereby all our problems will be solved.

Priscilla," announced the damsel's sister, "will marry the nabob. Once they are engaged, and the marriage contracts are signed and sealed and our family connections securely tied, I shall request of her fiancé a loan of fifteen thousand to pay Townsend's gambling debts."

Oblivious to the trampling beneath her feet of what in normal summers would have been a carpet of bluebells, but was now only a field of struggling green sprinkled here and there with a hint of blue, Madeline hurried down the sloping land through a wood of centuries-old walnut and oak trees. She had walked briskly for the first mile, outrage lending speed to her limbs, but a stitch in the side slowed her pace for the last quarter mile. Her destination, the one place that always calmed her anger, always refreshed her soul; it was the gently flowing brook that served as partial boundary line between Wybourne and the Balenger estate. Just north of the widest bend of the brook was a sheltered bower she had always thought of as her special place. To be there, alone—save for the water, the birds, and the woodland creatures—always brought her peace.

And if she ever needed peace, she needed it now, at this moment.

How dare they! How dare they plan Priscilla's future without a moment's thought for the child's own wishes, or for what would bring her happiness. A stranger might be forgiven for assuming the Wycliffs had but one child, so quick were her parents to sacrifice their oldest and their youngest for the sake of the middle daughter.

When she heard Bella's cavalier arranging of Priscilla's life, Madeline had battled an almost overpowering urge to dash into the adjoining parlor and snatch a fistful of titian locks from her sister's head. That urge might have won over had her father not chosen that very moment to stomp into the house and shout loudly enough to be heard all the way to the attic rooms, "Where is my daughter? I know she is here. Where are you, my *bella* Bella?"

Squealing with delight, Arabella ran from the room, presumably to throw herself into her father's arms; Mrs. Wycliff followed her daughter at a slightly more decorous pace. Once the parlor was abandoned, Madeline had taken the opportunity to escape, opening the casement window and scurrying through it, walking quickly down the footpath that separated the neat kitchen garden from the cutting garden long gone to seed, and then hastening to the woods beyond.

Now, her breathing labored and the stitch shooting little daggers into her side, she walked the final few yards that would put her at the brook and the series of flat, pinkish stepping-stones that allowed her to cross over to the far bank.

Strictly speaking, once she attained the other side of the water, she was trespassing. However, that was a minor point. Since there had not been a bailiff at Balenger Hall for twenty years or more, no one had ever questioned her right to be there.

Only once had Madeline seen anyone in the vicinity of her special place, and she had been a young girl at the time. The interloper—a short, heavyset gypsy—had stood in the middle of the warm, knee-deep water, his hands cupped together, attempting to catch a fish. Alone, and fearing the consequences of an encounter with a poacher caught in the act, Madeline had turned and run back to Wybourne as fast as her feet would carry her. Later, afraid her mother might forbid her to return to the brook, Madeline had kept the discovery of the gypsy to herself. She had encountered no one since that time.

Today she traversed the stepping-stones with more

care than was usual, owing to the fact that she had not stopped to change from slippers to walking boots, but by slow, guarded steps, she arrived on the far bank without a mishap. She eyed the little enclosure that was formed by low-hanging greenwood boughs, entwined with stinging nettle grown fully two meters high, and filled in by wild blackberry brambles; but she decided against her bower for the moment, choosing instead a likely spot on the fern-covered bank to sit and catch her breath.

This particular July day, in the summer that seemed destined never to come, the sun shone warmly, and Madeline meant to take full advantage of its rays, especially since she had also failed to acquire a cloak before fleeing the house.

Caring little for the possible damage to her old morning gown—the blue stripes so faded, the nainsook appeared very nearly all white—she plopped down on the grass. After several deep, steadying breaths, she allowed the tranquillity of the softly gurgling water to soothe her angry thoughts. Minute by minute the lulling sounds of the brook, accompanied by the music of a nearby wren whose bubbly warble was being challenged by the sweet song of a distant throstle, began to work their magic upon her. Her vexation began to ebb.

No good could come of nurturing resentment. She had learned that years ago when other inequities had sent her running pell-mell to this place. She lived the life to which she had been born, and railing against it for very long did harm only to her inner self. After all, how could she complain?

In comparison to the struggles of the cottagers and the laborers in Little Easton—hardworking people whose lives had grown more harsh as a result of the war, and yet had not improved in the thirteen months since Napoleon fell in defeat at Waterloo—Madeline's life must appear a fairy dream. Did she not have a sound roof over her head and plenteous food on the table?

Still she longed for something more.

With her knees pulled up to her chest, her arms wrapped around her limbs, Madeline let her mind wander, and as always, dreams of adventure—the fantasies of her childhood—flitted through her thoughts. How she longed for excitement. For travel. And for that greatest adventure of all, love.

She was five and twenty, and only in her mind had she visited those exotic places she longed to see . . . Paris, Venice, the pyramids of Cairo. Her only actual trips were those to Little Easton, the market town some five miles to the west, and Glastonbury, the larger town to the south where she and Bella had attended the Misses Zubers' Female Academy. And it looked as if those two placid locations might well be the extent of her travels.

As for her hopes of finding love and happiness, that fantasy, too, seemed less and less likely as time passed. Recently her mother had dropped a few rather broad hints that Madeline should accept her single state as permanent and begin wearing caps. In this one thing, however, she had rebelled, unwilling to sound the death knell for her dreams of one day meeting the soul for whom her soul waited.

Soul mates! She sounded as foolish as her young sister.

With a deprecating shrug of her shoulders, Madeline called herself a romantic fool, advising herself to leave off dreams of mythical soul mates. Striving to be obedient to these practical instructions, she looked about her for something to distract her thoughts, and happily she spied a pale yellow primrose close to the water's edge. Enchanted by the sight of the delicate blossom, valiantly living its life long after spring had passed it by, she determined to draw close enough to enjoy the flower's fragrance.

Stepping cautiously, lest she lose her footing on the moist ferns, Madeline descended the sloping bank. She had almost reached the primrose when, as if from nowhere, a man stepped out of the woods and stopped at that spot where she had sat only moments ago.

"What the deuce are you doing?" he demanded.

Startled, Madeline turned quickly. Too quickly; for as she turned she felt her feet slip beneath her. Though she flailed her arms about in hopes of maintaining her balance, she knew even as she did so that her case was hopeless.

Realizing her plight, the man rushed forward to aid her, and for just an instant she thought perhaps he might reach her in time. He did not.

With a feeling of total unreality, Madeline pitched backward into the brook. Although she knew the water was not dangerously deep, still she panicked when she collided with the sandy bottom and felt the sudden rush of water cover her head.

Within seconds of her submersion, a pair of strong hands lifted her out of the stream and set her on her feet. While she coughed and sputtered, ridding her burning lungs of what felt like an entire ocean, long powerful fingers grasped her upper arms, holding her securely.

Once her coughing had subsided and her breathing grew more regular, her rescuer asked, "Are you all right?"

Concerned only with her skirts, which had expanded like a hot air balloon and seemed to be billowing about her knees in a most unladylike manner, she stepped away from the stranger and began pushing at the offending garment.

"Better let me help you out of there," he suggested.

For one startled instant Madeline thought he referred to her wet dress. However, after a moment's reflection, she reasoned that he meant out of the brook. Blushing madly at her missishness, she allowed the man to take her hand and assist her from the water and up the bank, a slow, painstaking task. Although caught in a battle of wills with the skirts that now wrapped themselves around her limbs like clinging vines, threatening to trip her at every step, she was fully aware of the man who helped her.

A tall man, he wore leather riding boots that had seen better days and fawn breeches that were now wet up to his rock-hard thighs. He wore neither coat nor cravat, and his water-speckled shirt revealed a wide, muscular back and broad, powerful shoulders. But what caught Madeline's attention was the jagged scar on the man's right forearm. Because his shirtsleeves had been cuffed and rolled halfway up his arms, she was able to view the entire scar, which zigzagged its way from just below his elbow down to the top of his thumb.

A shiver ran through her. *What in heaven's name did a man do to receive such a scar?* It was not the result of some common farm accident; of that she was certain.

At first she had thought the stranger was a gypsy, fooled by the swarthiness of his skin. But now, looking at the thick, sun-streaked brown hair that was innocent of pomades or other artifices of the barber's trade, she realized that his skin color, like his hair, was the result of years spent out of doors. And if she was any judge, those years had been spent in hard labor; for in addition to his muscular physique, his hands gave testimony of his past.

Unlike the soft, smooth hands of the men who partnered her at the monthly assemblies in Little Easton, this man's hands were strong and work-roughened. Whoever and whatever he was, he was no pampered gentleman.

When they reached level ground, she eased her hand

from his. "Thank you," she said. "I feel such a ninny-hammer to have—"

Whatever she had meant to say, it fled from her mind the moment he turned and looked at her, impaling her with the most amazing gray eyes she had ever seen. Gray made even more remarkable due to the contrast with his tanned skin. Small, almost invisible lines fanned out from around those eyes, a result, most likely, from years of squinting into the sun.

Logic told her that the man must have a legitimate reason for being there. But logic being such a soft-spoken fellow, Madeline paid him no heed, her thoughts leaping to the quite fantastical notion that she had come face-to-face with a pirate.

While she studied the stranger, he studied her, looking her up and down, from the hair that had tumbled from its twist on top of her head and now hung soddenly about her shoulders, to the ruined slippers on her feet. As his gaze traveled her length, lingering for several moments on the dress that clung to her person like a second skin, a knowing and rather disturbingly male smile pulled at the corners of his mouth.

Feeling the heat of embarrassment suffuse her face, Madeline was about to give him the verbal dressing-down he so richly deserved, when suddenly a spark straight from Beelzebub lit his eyes and he threw back his head and laughed.

"What an astounding place this is, to be sure," he said once the deep, rich laughter had faded and only the devilish light remained in those gray eyes. "Fifteen years I sailed the seas without once sighting anything more wondrous than a pod of silver whales. And what happens the moment I give up the sea and return to land? I stroll by a shallow brook and discover a beautiful mermaid."

Chapter 2

"You are a sailor?" the woman asked, her face alight with wonder. "I was not so very wrong after all."

"Your pardon, miss?"

"Oh, nothing, just a fanciful thought I had."

Blushing rosily, the woman lifted her arms, caught handfuls of her thick brown hair, then began to pull the damp locks up to the top of her head where she twisted them into a knot. While she tucked the end strands beneath the knot to secure it, Philip Balenger let his gaze rest upon the bodice of her dress where the water had transformed the thin, faded material into something transparent and altogether alluring.

She was a woman well past her first blush of youth, but she would be coloring in earnest if she had any idea what she was revealing to him with every movement of her arms.

Demme, but her body is beautiful! And after looking into her sky blue eyes, Philip would bet half his fortune the nymph had no idea just how tantalizingly feminine she was.

"I am excessively obliged to you," she began, her voice calm, her manner unpretentious, "for likening me to a mermaid. If I could be any creature in nature, I believe that would be my choice."

Intrigued by this admission he said, "You have ignored the whole, miss. I likened you to a beautiful mermaid."

Again the color tinted the clear, satin skin of her cheeks. What a strange combination of maturity and innocence existed in this trespasser upon his land. When she did not run away the moment she was free of the water, as he would expect any proper young lady to do, he had been momentarily suspicious that she might be another of those females who had so relentlessly pursued him in London. And yet, there was no mistaking the lack of guile in her eyes.

Of course, there was always the possibility that she had not yet heard that the wealthy India nabob had returned to his ancestral seat. If she knew who he really was, she might be employing all manner of arts to attract him; like the ladies of the *ton*, charmed by his money. Yet, for some perverse reason, Philip did not want to think of this mermaid with the innocent eyes and the entrancing curves as just another gold-digging female.

"Because you were so kind to rescue me," she said, bringing his thoughts back to the moment, "allow me to return the favor by offering you a warning."

"A warning?"

"Yes. I think it only fair that I do so. You being a sailor just returned from the sea, you may not know that the owner of this property is expected to take up residence any day now. So if you were thinking of fishing these waters, you might wish to reconsider. Poachers, if caught, face prosecution and perhaps even deportation."

She was so serious, the little mermaid, that Philip found himself unable to resist the urge to tease her a little. "I shall not get caught! Although I thank you for the warning, I have eluded some of the most bloodthirsty brigands who ever set sail, and I do not suppose the local squire would give me any cause for alarm."

Far from being appalled by what she heard, her eyes grew wide with—what was it? Fascination?

"Then you *are* a pirate," she breathed.

He feigned insult. "If you please, miss. A buccaneer."

The woman giggled most delightfully.

"I collect, miss, that you are not frightened by the prospect of being in the presence of a buccaneer."

"Frightened?" She shook her head, and one of the carefully tucked stands worked free of her topknot and tumbled once again to her shoulder. To Philip's surprise, he was obliged to stop himself from reaching out to test the silkiness of that tress between his fingers. "No. I am not frightened," she continued. "Though, in all probability it denotes some sort of deficiency in my character. However, owing to the fact that pir—that is to say, buccaneers, do not come in my way very often, I should not wish to waste the opportunity by acting the coward."

Philip made the discovery that it was still possible to be surprised by someone. "I assure you, miss, there are not many who would look upon such a meeting as an opportunity."

"Oh, but I should." She paused for a moment. When she spoke again, her voice held a wistful quality. "Only think of the adventures a pirate must—"

"Buccaneer," he said, correcting her again.

She smiled at his reprimand, and he wondered if she knew how pretty she was. Somehow he doubted it.

"Only think," she said, "of the many adventures a *buccaneer* must have had, and the fascinating stories he could tell."

"I doubt you would find them so." Philip had difficulty keeping his face straight when he saw the disappointment in hers. "Quite vulgar, the tales would be, miss. And not fit for the ears of a well-bred lady."

"As though I would care for that," she said, "if only

he would tell me of the places he had been. The people he had seen. I have often thought that a sailor's life must be wonderfully full."

"More often short than full."

Philip heard the bitterness in his voice, a bitterness that had not lessened even though it had been fifteen years since the lad he once was had fallen victim to the press gangs and found himself aboard his first *East Indiaman*. No. The life had not been wonderfully full. What it had been was hard, and harder—with any misdemeanor calling forth a flogging, seamen succumbing right and left to fluxes and scurvy, and the least of the hardships the ever-present weevils in the bread and the green scum on the drinking water. But he doubted the lady would wish to hear of those adventures.

His bitter memories must have shown on his face, for his prize from the brook began making some excuse about needing to return to her home.

"And where is that?" he inquired, wanting to detain her a little longer. "If you are not truly an inhabitant of the deep, one can only assume you reside somewhere upon terra firma."

"My father's lands begin at the brook's other bank." After waving vaguely in that direction, she graciously offered him her hand, as though they had just been introduced. "I am Miss Wycliff, of Wybourne."

"Your servant, Miss Wycliff." Taking her hand in his, he lifted her fingers to his lips. Her skin felt incredibly soft, and without meaning to, he let his lips linger a moment longer than was proper. "I am Philip Bal—" He stopped, suddenly loath to reveal his identity and risk seeing that calculating look his name had elicited in London. Instead he said, "I am Philip, the buccaneer."

For all Madeline heard, he might have called himself Father Christmas. With his lips pressed against her fingers, she lost all her faculties save the sense of touch. The breath caught in her throat. Her heart seemed to stop its rhythmic beat. Her entire life force seemed focused upon the feel of his warm lips; and in that brief moment she experienced a shimmering of her flesh, a tingling as though her skin had suddenly awakened from a long sleep. Startled by this physical awareness, she eased her hand from his and put it behind her back, unwilling to look at it for fear it bore some evidence of her response. "I must be going," she said, hoping her voice did not convey the agitation of her senses.

"If I should happen this way again," he said, "say tomorrow, would I find you here?"

"Oh, no. I do not think—" *Again!* Had she heard him right? "You cannot mean you are staying here?"

"Yes. At the Hall."

"Balenger Hall?"

"I . . . er . . . the Hall is in need of work."

Madeline could not believe she had forgotten all about the scheme to marry her youngest sister to the wealthy owner of Balenger Hall; she assumed the dunking in the brook must have washed the subject from her mind. Now, however, that memory came rushing back, and with it some of the anger she had felt earlier. "You are working for the nabob?"

"In a manner of speaking. Anytime the nabob wants to be certain a thing is done right, he sends me to do the job."

Anytime? So this was an acquaintance of some duration. Not wishing to pass up this opportunity to discover something of the nabob's character, she said, "I collect you have known him for some time."

"The nabob? Oh, yes. Since he was a lad."

Madeline swallowed, ashamed of herself for what she

was about to do, encourage an employee to gossip about his employer. "Will you tell me something of him?"

From the slight raising of his eyebrows—a gesture haughty enough to shame a duke—Madeline could tell the buccaneer was disinclined to answer questions. Nevertheless, she was determined not to cry craven and leave before he told her what she needed to know.

"Believe me, I have no wish to pry into the nabob's personal life, so you may rest easy on that head. All I need to know is if he is the kind of gentleman who would make a good husband for a young and innocent girl."

The eyebrows lifted again, though his question was spoken softly. "You?"

Madeline felt the heat of embarrassment in her face, but honesty compelled her to admit that by her own prying, she had opened herself to such catechism. Swallowing her pride she said, "Five and twenty hardly qualifies me as a young girl. I inquire on behalf of my sister."

"And she would be . . ."

"Priscilla. She is but seventeen years old, still a girl by anyone's measure."

"And you wish Miss Priscilla to marry the nabob?"

"No. I do not!"

Forcing herself to recapture her lost composure, Madeline continued, "That is to say, I do not wish it unless Priscilla should wish it. However, that is nothing to the point, for my sister has not yet made his acquaintance, never mind forming a lasting attachment. But should she meet him and find him not to her taste, then no matter what arguments Bella and Mama shall put forth, I will not let Priscilla be coerced into marriage."

"That's the ticket! By all means, you must not let Miss Priscilla be swayed by Mama and . . . Bella, did you say?"

"Yes, Bel—" Madeline stopped, noting that the play-ful look had returned to his gray eyes. "I perceive that you are making sport of me, but I wish you would not. I am in earnest. If the nabob is a worthy man, I would not wish to put an impediment in Priscilla's way, for I know all too well that there are few eligible men in the vicin-ity. But above all other considerations, I desire to see my sister happily established. So if you know ought of—"

"Seventeen, was it?" He appeared to be giving the matter some reflection. "Nay," he answered finally, "hint her away, Miss Wycliff. The nabob is no fit partner for such a young lady."

"Not?"

"Not." He sighed dramatically. "It distresses me to re-veal all to you, but the Balenger is a regular rascal. A rogue. A bounder. A ne'er-do-well. A knave. A—a—"

"A scoundrel?" she added helpfully, not immune to his teasing manner.

"Aye, that, too. As am I myself. We are two of a kind, you might say."

Madeline chuckled. "Coming it a bit too brown, I be-lieve. For you are, by your own admission, a buccaneer. And if my sister—my other sister, Lady Townsend—is to be believed, the nabob is a gentleman received in all the best homes in London."

"Fine feathers make fine birds." Having said this, the teasing light left his eyes and a rueful expression showed on his angular face. "Or more to the point, golden guineas make acceptable gentlemen."

Wishing to be clear regarding this subject, Madeline asked earnestly, "Are you saying the nabob is not a gen-tleman?"

He answered with equal earnestness. "I spoke only the truth when I said the Balenger and I were two of a kind. We are as like as four pence to a groat. Neither of us gentlemen, and neither of us fit husbands for young ladies of tender years."

Madeline shivered, though whether she reacted to clothing that had progressed from cold and clammy to clinging sheets of ice, or whether from the revelation about the nabob, she did not know. Whichever it was, she knew she must find dry clothes soon or risk an ague, and she needed time to think about what she had learned.

As if reading her thoughts, her informant said, "Swim on home, little mermaid, for I perceive it is time you returned to your own kind. Do not tarry here. 'Tis a cold and unforgiving world for the unwary."

Madeline chose to enter the house through the door to the kitchen rather than go around to the front and risk being seen by her mother. Considering the sodden condition of her dress and shoes, she blessed her good fortune in finding the housekeeper, the maid of all work, and the scullery maid sitting beside the warm cookstove, shelling peas.

"Miss Maddy!" the housekeeper shrieked. "Whatever has happened?"

"The saints preserve us," begged the scullery.

Shivering, Madeline drew near the warmth of the stove. "I fell in the brook, Jinksie. Could you spare Tess to help me get out of these wet things? I will send her back to you within five minutes."

"You'll do no such thing, Miss Maddy." Mrs. Jinks moved with a speed that belied her more than ample girth, quitting her comfortable rocking chair and hurrying to the door, where she lifted a woolen shawl from off one of the pegs. "Here, miss, put this around your shoulders for the nonce." After doing the job herself, the good woman turned to her two minions. "Tess!"

The young maid bobbed a curtsy. "Yes, Mrs. Jinks."

"Run up to Miss Madeline's room and get a fire started, there's a good girl. As soon as you assist her out of these wet clothes and into her wrapper, you come back down and help Maeve take up the hip bath. The water should be heated by that time."

"No, really, Jinksie," Madeline protested, "you three have more than enough work to do without waiting upon me hand and foot. I cannot allow y—"

"Pish and tosh. You just let old Jinksie be the judge of what can and cannot be allowed here in her own kitchen."

The housekeeper gave Tess a nod that sent the girl scurrying up the back stairs to do as she had been instructed. "It's little enough I can do for you, Miss Maddy, and that's a fact. So, if you please, I'll hear no more argufying about it. No more than you would listen to my protests last year when my little nevvy was run down by the carter's wagon, and you sold the garnet brooch that was all you had left of your grandma's things to see the boy's legs was fixed up proper like."

Mrs. Jinks lifted the hem of her apron to her eyes for a quick swipe before giving Madeline a gentle shove toward the stairs. "Now you go on up, miss, and see you soak in that tub a good long time. Then you hop right into your bed and pull the covers up snug and cozy. Jinksie'll send you up a tray with some hot broth as soon as you're settled."

"But, I—"

"Hush now, do. Let somebody pamper you for once. It's precious little cosseting you've had, and that's a fact. Now off with you, and if you want to ward off the effects of the dousing in the brook, don't be leaving your bed again until morning."

Although Madeline did as she was bid and let herself be cosseted, she woke late the next morning not as re-

freshed as she should have been. She credited the lack of
restful slumber in small part to the unfavorable information she had discovered concerning the character of the
nabob, but in greater part to the dream she'd had involving herself and her swarthy informant.

Closing her eyes against the sunlight that peeped
through the carelessly drawn curtains of her chamber
window, sending stripes of gold stretching from the foot
of her half tester bed, across the braided rug upon the
floor, to end at the peach-washed wall behind the plain
oak dressing table, she relived that disturbing dream.

In the timeless, boundaryless world of illusion, an exultant and starry-eyed Madeline had stood at the bow of
a handsome schooner whose tall white sails were filled
almost to bursting. While the ship glided over the ocean
waves as effortlessly as skaters on a frozen pond, soft,
salty spray kissed Madeline's cheek and gentle trade
winds blew her hair, which hung loose and free, like a
mermaid's. Standing behind her, his strong, tanned arms
wrapped around her waist, his chin resting against her
head, was—

No! It was not him.

Pulling the covers up to her neck, as though bits of
linen and wool would shield her from her own thoughts,
Madeline attempted to reshape the vivid dream.

In vain she tried to convince herself that the man in
whose arms she had stood so contentedly was just some
nebulous heroic archetype—someone she had conjured
up—a person no more real than the schooner itself. But
never a self-deceiver, she finally admitted that one of
those tanned arms, whose solidity and strength she had
so wantonly enjoyed, was branded with a jagged scar. A
scar whose owner she knew full well.

Castigating herself as a wet goose, a romantic fool, a
moonling, and every other name she could think of, she

wondered if her mama might not be right to suggest she begin wearing caps. Obviously none but an old maid past praying for would be dreaming of a man she had met only for a brief moment in a wood. And not even a gentleman. A laborer of some kind.

Madeline closed her eyes against the shudder that overtook her, recalling the quite unpleasant epithet sometimes used by ladies of her class to refer to women—romantically unfulfilled women—who aligned themselves with men of a lower social class.

"Stop it!" she ordered, tossing the covers back and sitting up in her bed. "He was a man—like any other—and you conversed with him for a brief time. What fault was there in that? Can a lady not be civil to a laborer? Must she turn up her nose and pretend a man does not exist simply because his physique is comely, his skin is tanned from the sun and the wind, and his gray eyes are alight with having lived life to the fullest?"

Receiving no answer to her admittedly democratic questions, she swung her feet to the floor, then strode to the sturdy oak clothespress, yanking open the door and snatching out stockings, drawers, shift, stays, and petticoat, donning each in turn without assistance.

Because of the constant lack of money in the Wycliff household, the ladies of the house did not enjoy the services of a personal maid. Therefore dressing oneself and one's own hair was a common occurrence, and one Madeline performed without thought, while still berating herself for remembering too well the feel of warm lips upon her fingers.

Thankfully this fruitless recollection was interrupted by the arrival of her younger sister, who burst into her room almost immediately after knocking upon the door.

"Madeline! You will never guess what has happened."

"No," she replied so calmly one might never have

supposed her to have been mooning over a quite ineligible person, "I would not. But, of course, I was never very good at guessing games."

"Well, even if you were good at them, you would never guess this." Stopping for breath, Priscilla scrutinized her sister, who sat at the dressing table. "Why are you wearing one of your good frocks?" Not waiting for an answer, she gave Madeline's shoulder a gentle push to turn the stool on which she sat and began doing up the hooks that had been left undone at the back of the dark blue jaconet frock. "Are you expecting a visitor?"

"I am expecting no one."

"Then why . . ." Bending to look at her sister in the looking glass, Priscilla said, "And you have fixed your hair differently. I must say it looks nice that way, with the tendrils falling softly around your face."

Madeline's gaze went quickly to the glass, glancing at her reflection almost as if seeing it for the first time. What in heaven's name had possessed her to take such special pains with her toilette? More than a little afraid that she knew the answer to that question, she snatched up her brush and began sweeping the tendrils snugly beneath the topknot.

"No! Do not." Priscilla took the brush from her sister's unresisting hand and tossed it onto the dressing table, then worked the tendrils loose again. "Leave them as they were, for you look quite pretty."

Blushing at the unaccustomed compliment, Madeline bade her sister tell her what had brought her bursting into her room.

"Oh, I almost forgot. Guess who is coming back to Little Easton." Giving Madeline no time to vouchsafe a reply, the youngest Wycliff continued, "And not just to the neighborhood, but right next door . . . to Balenger Hall."

Realizing she could not disclose her knowledge of the nabob's imminent arrival without revealing her rather reprehensible act of eavesdropping, Madeline feigned ignorance. "I am all out of guesses, and pray you will inform me soon, for I am ravenously hungry and wish to go down to breakfast."

"It is the Balenger heir. The grandson. And you will never guess what else he is."

"There is more?"

"Yes, much more. And I vow, it is too, too exciting. He is a nabob. Enormously wealthy, so Bella says. And unmarried."

Madeline looked up at her sister. "Do you find that of interest, then? His being a bachelor."

"Do not be absurd, Maddy. Naturally I find that of interest. As should you."

"Me?"

"Certainly. For Bella says he is quite handsome, in addition to being as rich as—as—whoever that rich king was from long ago. You know the one I mean."

"I collect you mean Croesus. Though I do not believe I ever heard that the Lydian king was particularly handsome."

"Do not toy with me, goose. The king was just rich. It is Mr. Balenger who is said to be both rich *and* handsome."

The young girl sighed. "I could almost wish he were not so old. Thirty, I think Bella said. But never mind, a man of thirty should do very nicely for you."

Chapter 3

"Me!"

Madeline looked into Priscilla's lovely, young face and knew a moment of such sisterly affection that she was forced to turn away from the girl's watchful eyes and pretend to check her coiffure in the looking glass.

Priscilla seemed not to notice. Laughing, she told her sister of the scene she had been privy to in the breakfast room. "It was so exquisitely droll. There was Mama, trying everything she could think of to wheedle Papa into delaying his trip to the race meet, in order to present himself at Balenger Hall to make the nabob's acquaintance. While Papa . . . Well, you can imagine Papa's responses to both suggestions."

"Now *that* I can guess, since nothing takes precedence over sport."

"Naturally. But Mama did not take defeat easily. All the time Papa was shoveling food into his mouth, his eyes never leaving his plate, she continued in her efforts to bring him to a realization of what he owed his family." A wicked light shown in the storyteller's angelic blue eyes. "Mama was in high form."

"Palpitations?"

"To be sure."

"Followed by a sinking spell?"

"Of a certainty. And this one accompanied by blurred

vision. When she called for her smelling salts and went into a swoon, Papa made his escape."

The sisters chuckled, in very good understanding of both their parents.

"But never mind that," Priscilla said, returning to the much more interesting topic of their soon-to-be neighbor. "I tell you, Maddy, this is fate. Only think of your being here, as yet unwed, at just the time the Balenger heir returns to take his place at the hall. Could anything be more perfect?" She winked unashamedly. "At least *I* think it perfect, for you could have a husband and an establishment of your own without having to move away, leaving me here alone. And since the nabob has pots of money, he could take you to someplace grand for your wedding trip. One of those strange, foreign places you are always reading about."

Madeline swallowed a rather sizable lump in her throat at her sister's unselfish plans. "But what of you, Priscilla?" From the damsel's dispassionate discussion of the nabob, it was obvious Mrs. Wycliff had said nothing to her youngest daughter about a possible betrothal between her and their new neighbor. "Would you not enjoy being the wife of a wealthy gentleman?"

"Well," the young girl answered after a moment's consideration, "I will not prevaricate and tell you that money means nothing to me, but I would not let the lack of it weigh against a gentleman for whom I had formed a lasting *tendre*.

"Of course," she added, "the gentleman I shall marry will not be *old*, like the nabob."

Much affected by this piece of information, Madeline said, "So you consider a gentleman of thirty too old for you."

Priscilla wrinkled her nose in distaste. "*Much* too old."

Having been apprised of her sister's feelings upon the matter, how could Madeline stand by and let the child be forced into a marriage that was distasteful to her? She could not. Not as long as she had breath in her body. That resolved, she decided to go to Balenger Hall to face the new heir, and to see just what manner of man he really was.

"Maddy, what a look you have on your face. So intense. Almost as if you were girding up to meet someone in battle."

"David meeting Goliath," she mumbled.

"I hope you are in jest."

Surprised that she had spoken her thoughts aloud, Madeline stood and gave her sister a quick hug. "Pay me no heed, for I am being nonsensical."

"No," Priscilla said, returning the hug, "you are never nonsensical. You are the most practical person I know."

Until yesterday Madeline would have agreed with that assessment, but since her tumble into the brook, she seemed to be giving in to all manner of fanciful notions. Not wishing to make these notions public, however, she kept her own counsel, merely mentioning that she had promised to call upon one or two of the basket weavers.

"Nothing is amiss, Priscilla, so do not worry. Instead do me a favor, please. While I have a bite of breakfast, go to the stable and ask Jem to get the gig ready."

Less than an hour later, Madeline climbed up into the gig, being careful to sit up straight to avoid snagging her Cambridge blue cloak on any of the half dozen broken canes in the back of the seat. Jem had harnessed Comet, the old roan gelding, who was anything but a speeding ball of fire, then left the gig at the front of the house, for his services had been needed to drive the landau. Mrs. Wycliff and Arabella were off to visit the rectory to pay their respects to the Hazlips, a circumstance that suited

Madeline very well, since it made it unnecessary for her to tell another falsehood regarding her destination.

Because Comet had long ago abandoned all inclination to trot or gallop, no matter what inducements or threats were employed by the person handling the ribbons, the two-mile drive to Balenger Hall needed a half hour. But Madeline used the time to good advantage, composing and rehearsing the speech she meant to use to gain entry to a house where she was acquainted with neither the owner nor his servants.

The road, a deep, rutted lane overhung with trees and bordered by ancient hedges thick with bindweed and thistle, was barely wide enough to allow two carts to pass. Fortunately Madeline met no other conveyances before she arrived at the gray stone entrance to the Balenger estate. She turned the plodding horse past the iron gate that had been closed for years but now stood open, and continued up the overgrown driveway toward the hall.

She had never seen the Hall up close and was surprised to discover a beautiful William and Mary country house; at least it would be beautiful once some attention was paid to it. Unlike Wybourne, which was a modest, gray stone manor house of only a dozen family rooms, the Hall was at least double that size in its central section, with a half dozen rooms in each of its two wings. Fashioned of red brick long since mellowed to pink, the well-proportioned building boasted numerous tall, leaded windows, a graceful, wide portico, and a heavy wooden door turned black with age.

Against the far corner of the house leaned a freshly whetted scythe. Apparently the tool had been abandoned recently, for large mounds of grass and weeds gave evidence that someone had been busy that morning.

Since no one came from the stables to assist her,

Madeline climbed down from the gig and draped the reins loosely over the splashboard, leaving Comet to graze to his heart's content among what remained of the tall grass.

Taking a deep breath to steady her nerves, she pushed the hood from her head, lifted the hem of her skirt and cloak, then approached the portico. The brass knocker was heavy in her hand. She raised it, letting it fall only once.

The door was opened almost the instant the knocker fell, leading Madeline to believe someone had been aware of her arrival from the first. As the door swung wide, the carefully rehearsed speech fled from Madeline's brain, like a rabbit suddenly come upon a hound. Except the man who opened the door was no hound, even though Madeline felt suspiciously like a frightened rabbit.

Before her stood a mahogany-skinned giant dressed in a knee-length white coat, which was buttoned over some type of yellow, gathered trousers. On his feet he wore fanciful slippers fashioned of soft leather and stitched with golden thread, and about his head he had wound a white turban that bore an enameled clip in the shape of a crescent moon.

After inclining his head in a bow that managed somehow to appear respectful without conveying the least subservience, the man merely stared at Madeline, a question in his midnight eyes.

She straightened as tall as she could, in hopes that it might bolster her confidence. "I am Mrs. Wycliff, of Wybourne," she informed him, "and I have come to see Mr. Balenger."

"Sahib in London," the giant informed her in his heavily accented English.

"But I thought—"

"Not here," he said.

Obviously considering the discussion at an end, the servant bowed briefly, then closed the heavy door, the resulting thud echoing like the boom of a cannon.

Madeline gasped, astonished at having a door closed in her face, while Comet took the loud noise even more personally, whinnying in fright. With the perverse logic of his kind, the gelding instantly turned and bolted down the driveway, the gig bouncing haplessly behind him. As though pursued by a league of banshees, he galloped at a speed he had not exhibited in a half dozen years.

Madeline dashed from beneath the portico. "Comet! Whoa, boy." The horse paid her no heed.

As he rounded the corner of the drive and disappeared from sight, Madeline stamped her foot in frustration. "Blast and double blast! Now how do I get home?"

There was only one answer to that query, *shank's mare*. Since occasional encounters with gypsies or vagrants made walking alone on the road out of the question, she looked about her for the most direct route to the boundary dividing the two properties. Her plan: to travel across the Balenger estate until she found the brook and the stepping-stones, then to cross the water to her father's property. Satisfied with this strategy, she strode eastward and very soon found herself on a gravel path that led her to the Balenger stable—a single-story, rectangular, brick building that wanted the services of a carpenter and a glazier.

"Here," called a deep voice from inside the building, "let me give you a hand with that."

Madeline stopped in mid-stride, not certain she wished to continue in that direction, for she had recognized the voice. It belonged to the buccaneer.

Standing some thirty yards from the entrance to the stable, she watched as one of the doors that hung drunkenly upon its hinges was suddenly lifted into place by two men. While the younger of the two held the door steady, the older—a stocky, middle-aged man dressed in corduroy breeches, a colored neckerchief, and a stout smock—hammered a fresh pin into the hinge. Philip was dressed much as he had been yesterday, in boots, breeches, and a lawn shirt, and as before, his shirtsleeves were rolled up past his elbows. While he strained beneath the weight of the door, his back to her, Madeline watched the play of his muscles, enjoying their superb shape, their magnificent symmetry.

"Good man," Philip said, swinging the door a short distance inward then repeating the swing outward. "That should do nicely. Now as to the other, perhaps we can—"

"Good day to you, miss," the man in the smock said, pulling the bill of his cap.

Philip turned quickly, his face set in angry lines, and for just a moment Madeline wished she had not come this way. Within seconds, however, the buccaneer's face lost its irritation, and as he walked toward her, his mouth relaxed and turned up at the corners.

"What is this?" he inquired quietly, his gaze taking a leisurely inventory of her person from her jean half boots all the way up to the tendrils Priscilla had combed around her face. "Have the seas all gone dry, that beautiful mermaids must now wander the land afoot?"

Though she knew she should reprimand him for such blatant flattery, somehow Madeline could not bring herself to do so. Instead she smiled and was rewarded for her forbearance by a warming look in his gray eyes, a look that started a wild fluttering in the general region of her ribs.

With no little difficulty, she finally found her voice. "My being afoot has nothing whatever to do with the sea, and everything to do with a vexatiously stupid horse who thought little of bolting at the first unusual sound and leaving me stranded."

"Ah, yes," Philip said, his voice conveying a suggestion of understanding, as between kindred spirits, "we creatures of the sea often find ourselves at a loss when dealing with landlubbers."

While he talked, he took her arm and led her over to a stone-mounting block and bade her be seated, which she did, with her feet on the bottom step of the block and her hands folded primly in her lap.

"And now," he said, "perhaps you will tell me how you happened to be at Balenger Hall when your horse decided to take himself off? Was there something in particular you wanted?"

"No. Yes." Madeline shook her head, loath to admit her breach of propriety in seeking his employer, a bachelor with whom she could claim not even the slightest acquaintance. "What I mean to say . . . that is . . ."

"I do admire a woman who knows her own mind."

Though she tried not to do so, Madeline could not help chuckling at his absurd observation, knowing full well she was acting like the veriest pea-goose.

"That is better," he said quietly, "for I would much rather hear you laugh."

Philip propped his foot on the step, obviously unaware that the toe of his boot touched the toe of her boot, and seemingly oblivious to the fact that his knee was very nearly touching her knee.

After placing his hand on his bent leg, he leaned forward and spoke softly, as if for her ears only, his voice lazy, his words teasing. "Did you know that when you laugh, your eyes fairly sparkle? They remind me of the clear blue waters of the Aegean when the noon sun catches the tip of a wave and kisses it with light."

Madeline felt that fluttering again, only this time it

seemed to have moved to her lungs and was playing havoc with her breathing. Aware that their conversation had taken a decidedly improper turn, she tried to quell the pleasure she experienced at his words, and in doing so, found herself blurting out her reason for having come to the Hall.

"Mama tried to get Papa to come over here to make the nabob's acquaintance, so that Priscilla could be introduced to his notice, only Papa was so disobliging as to ignore Mama's request and take himself off to a race meet. For my part, I am glad he did so, for when I asked Priscilla if she might, in fact, be entertaining hopes in that direction, she said she was not."

"A wise young lady, is Miss Priscilla. I collect she is of higher principles than to wed for money. Does she regard the Balenger's gold with aversion?"

Madeline shook her head. "No, not his gold. When I asked her if she would like to be the wife of a wealthy gentleman, she said she had no objection to wealth."

"Then what explanation, if I may be so bold as to inquire, did she give for her lack of interest? Had it anything to do with what I told of the Balenger's character?"

"No. Priscilla said the nabob was too old."

Philip was seized by a coughing fit and had, perforce, to move away from the mounting block until he had recovered. "Did you say, 'Too old'?"

"That is correct. But you must remember that Priscilla is only just turned seventeen, and to her, thirty seems a prodigiously great age."

"And what of you? What think you of that hoary accumulation of years?"

"I? You will collect that I am five and twenty. To me, thirty seems the very age a man ought to be, if he had any say in the matter."

"You relieve my mind," he said dryly.

"Well, I hope it may be so. Though I fail to see what difference my opinion should make."

"Within the sennight," he said, "I shall turn *one* and thirty."

"Oh, no," she said, pressing her lips together to stop them from smiling. "Permit me to offer you my felicitations on your coming anniversary."

"Do not try to turn me up sweet, my girl. Not now. Not after informing me that *thirty* is old."

"But you have mistaken the matter. For in that particular instance I was relating my *sister's* views upon the subject. And now that I know the facts as they pertain to you, I will take leave to alter *my* view. I now perceive that *one* and thirty is the exact age a man should choose to be."

"There can, of course, be no two opinions on that."

Madeline almost choked. "Allow me to inform you that you are a blackguard to—"

"I told you that yesterday."

"A blackguard," she continued, "to make me laugh when I have come here on a serious matter."

"But I distinctly remember telling you that I *like* to hear you laugh."

"Which you should not!"

"On that, we must remain of two opinions."

Allowing her no time for retort, he continued, "As for this business about Miss Priscilla and the nabob, you may trust me when I tell you that Balenger is never interested in very young ladies. In fact, one of the reasons he fled town was to quit the company of young females who did *not* find him too old. Or so they and their mamas would have him believe."

"Fled? You speak in the past tense. Yet his butler—or whoever that giant in the turban may be—said the nabob was still in London."

Philip busied himself with brushing away a smut from the knee of his breeches. "Singh had the right of it. Mine was a slip of the tongue."

"Oh."

In the silence that followed, Madeline became conscious of the time. Perceiving that it was probably an hour or more since she had left Wybourne, and afraid she may have lingered overlong in Philip's company, she rose and then stepped down from the mounting block. "I should not have detained you, for you have a job of work to do. I must be going."

"Must you?" he asked warmly, making it difficult for her to remember that she had no business standing about enjoying what a casual observer might easily misconstrue as flirtatious bantering.

And enjoy it she had. No point in denying the obvious. Never mind that she was a lady, and as such ought not to be encouraging such familiarity from a laborer.

That he was precisely the sort of man she wished to encourage was just another of fate's capricious little jokes.

When she vouchsafed no denial of her intent to leave, Philip said, "I will see you home."

"No, please. There is no need. I can quite easily walk to the brook without—"

He reached out and touched the tip of his finger to her lips. "Shh. I wish you will be guided by me in this instance."

Any woman with a modicum of common sense would have turned and walked away. But the moment Philip touched her, making her heart thump as though it had every intention of leaping from her body, any claim Madeline had to being a woman of common sense disappeared.

"Please," he said. "Wait here. I will be but a moment."

He walked to the stable and said something to the workman in the smock; then, within little more than a minute, he returned, followed by the workman who led a large, beautifully proportioned Arab, its coat a shining ebony. The horse was saddled and eager for an outing, prancing about and bobbing his massive, dark head against the constraint of the tightly held rein.

Madeline gasped. "I cannot ride that! I am, at best, an indifferent rider. Believe me, I would be totally unable to control such an animal."

"Do not be concerned about controlling the gelding," Philip said.

Madeline mistrusted the light in his eyes, but she had no time to question it before he put his hands on either side of her waist and lifted her onto the mounting block, as easily as though she weighed no more than a couple of stones. With his hands still on her waist, he smiled up at her in a way that quite stole her breath. "The animal you need to worry about keeping in line is me."

Having issued his warning, he turned and took the reins from the workman, then mounted the horse in one smooth, easy motion. After allowing the gelding a couple of turns around the yard to vent his freshness, Philip drew him close to the mounting block. Before Madeline knew what he was about, Philip reached out and wrapped his arm around her waist and lifted her onto the horse, settling her before him.

"Now," he said, "will you be adventurous and let the wind blow through your hair, or do you want a moment to adjust your hood for anonymity, in case someone should see you in the company of a buccaneer?"

With her back flush against his broad chest and his muscular arm wrapped snugly around her waist, it was not her hood that needed adjusting, it was her breathing.

"I . . . I should like to feel the wind in my hair," she replied.

No point in telling him that she had worn this cloak for the last four years, and that every female in the village of Little Easton could name its owner if it were found lying abandoned in the road.

Madeline was practically sitting in Philip's lap, and though she could do nothing to keep her arms from resting against his forearm, she vowed to hold her hands tightly clasped before her and not touch him any more than was necessary. Like so many good plans, that one went astray. The moment Philip tapped the horse with his heels, the animal bounded forward, obliging Madeline to grasp his forearm with both her hands to keep her neck from being snapped like a twig.

She would not have believed she could be any more aware of the man, held against him as she was, in the circle of his arm, but Madeline was soundly disabused of that notion the instant she touched him. She had not reckoned on the jolt of pleasure that shot through her body when her hands gripped his forearm and felt the warmth of his bare skin and the ripple of muscles beneath that skin.

"Comfortable?" he asked as he drew the horse to a manageable trot.

Unable to speak, Madeline merely nodded her head.

"Good girl. At this pace, we should need no more than fifteen minutes to reach Wybourne."

Fifteen minutes! Madeline would never endure a quarter hour of this closeness. Not without making a complete fool of herself.

To give her thoughts a new direction, away from the twelve plus stone of muscular male behind her, Madeline concentrated on the gelding's black mane. From the mane, her gaze traveled to the reins, and from there to

Philip's right arm and to the long, jagged scar that ran the length of his forearm.

She knew she should not ask the question that had been on her mind since she first met him, but she needed something to divert her thoughts from his nearness. "How did you receive that scar?"

"Fighting a press-gang."

"A press—" Madeline was obliged to take a deep breath. The very words struck fear in her heart. Even though she had never set eyes on those bands of kidnappers who roamed the docks, preying upon the unwary, she knew of their practice of knocking men senseless, then selling them into servitude aboard any ship willing to pay the price.

"May it come to pass," she said, "that all press-gangs receive their just desserts!"

"A sentiment with which I heartily agree."

"Just so," she replied. "For 'tis no more than slavery to take men against their will and force them into a life aboard ship."

"True. But you must know that if it were not for the press-gangs, half the ships of the world would go unmanned."

"Perhaps that is the circumstance, but impressing is still a barbaric practice. And as long as it is allowed to continue, it diminishes the honor of every country involved."

When he offered no further comment, she inquired, "How ever did you make your escape from the gang?"

His answer, though softly spoken, was edged with bitterness. "I did not."

Chapter 4

"You were impressed?" Madeline felt chilled despite the warmth of her cloak. "When was that?"

"Many years ago. I was only fourteen at the time, but quite a strapping lad. I believe they mistook me for a man."

"Fourteen. Oh, Philip. You poor, poor boy."

The sincere concern in her voice caught him off guard. Over the years he had developed defenses against cruelty, avarice, and just plain meanness, but Philip was unprepared for sympathy. It attacked him in a vulnerable spot—a spot he had thought much too scarred to be pierced.

"I survived," he said, more for his own benefit than for hers. "And look at me now. I am back in the land of my birth. I have a fine horse to take me wherever I wish to go. And I number among my acquaintances a lovely lady who likes the feel of the wind in her hair. What more could a man ask?"

She seemed not to hear his words. "Is that when you met the nabob? How you came to know him?"

"You could say that. I certainly discovered what manner of man he was during that three-year stint."

Her voice held an angry sharpness. "Were you impressed aboard one of his ships?"

"Nay. The Balenger had no ships at that time. Only think, lass, he and I are much of an age."

"Of course," she said, relief in her tone, "what was I thinking. Besides, he is a gentleman."

"As to that, calling him a gentleman may be going overboard a mite, for you will recollect that I told you he is a rogue. Furthermore, by definition, a gentleman is a man who does not maintain himself by the sweat of his brow. Not so the Balenger. He has had to earn his keep. Toiled long and hard, he has. This I know for a fact."

"But he is a nabob. Are not nabobs always regarded as gentlemen?"

"Ah, the Englishman and his measuring rod. There can be no understanding it. If a man earns his wealth honestly, in a business in the city or the village, he smells of the shop. But let that same man amass his fortune outside the British Isles, and no matter how disreputable his methods, he is deemed a gentleman."

Madeline did not attempt to argue the inconsistencies of the English mind. "Surely there is more to a gentleman than his fortune, or how and where he acquired it."

"In truth, there should be. In fact . . . Ah, well, facts have a way of shaping themselves to fit the situation."

Philip slowed the gelding to a walk. A more leisurely pace would make conversation easier, as well as extending the amount of time he could spend in the company of his fascinating companion. Unfortunately his plans were thwarted by an antiquated carriage that was approaching from the rear, rapidly closing the gap between them. The vehicle's wheels rattled noisily while the horses' hooves clopped loudly upon the uneven road.

"Is there a place in this lane wide enough to allow a carriage to pass?" he asked.

"No. I am afraid the hedges—" She leaned forward enough to peer around him, obliging him to tighten his arm around her small waist. When she stiffened, however, he knew her rigidity had nothing to do with his boldness.

"Blast! It is Jem and the landau."

"Am I to assume you do not wish to be seen by this Jem?"

She shook her head. "It is the passengers in the landau. Mama and my sister."

"Miss Priscilla?"

"Bella."

With reasons of his own for not wanting to be seen by her sister, Lady Townsend, Philip pulled Madeline tightly against him and kicked his heels into the gelding's flanks, causing the Arab to break into a gallop. Within mere seconds they had left the carriage behind.

Madeline might be in an indifferent rider, but Philip was a master handler, and after the initial shock of the sudden movement, she gave herself up to the enjoyment of the ride. She felt as if they flew, so smoothly did the horse travel and so quickly did the scenery pass by. Too soon the gates of Wybourne appeared in the foreground.

When she pointed her arm to the left, Philip turned the four-legged flyer in that direction, and in a matter of moments they were bounding up the carriageway, the house straight ahead.

"Which way?" he yelled.

Turning so that her face was close to his, she shouted, "Around to the back of the house."

He followed her directions, encouraging the Arab to greater speed. When they neared the back entrance, Philip pulled the horse up, instantly dismounting and lifting Madeline down. "Hurry inside," he said. "Perhaps they may not have seen you."

Madeline did as he bade her and moved quickly to the door. At the threshold, however, she turned to watch

Philip ride away toward the wood and the brook that divided the lands of Wybourne from those of Balenger Hall. He and the horse moved as one, and Madeline experienced a stab of regret that he had left her here and gone on without her.

When man and horse were no longer in sight, swallowed up by the thick stand of oak and walnut trees, Madeline entered the kitchen and closed the heavy wooden door. Knowing her hair was blown by the wind, and fearing her eyes would betray the thrill she had experienced galloping down the road, with Philip holding her safely against him, she mumbled a brief greeting to the startled scullery maid, then sped up the back stairs to her room.

The inevitable summons came a scant ten minutes later. In those minutes, Madeline hurriedly tossed her cloak onto the bed, pressed a damp cloth to her flushed face, then snatched up her brush and tried what she could to tame the windblown strands into submission beneath her topknot.

"Maddy?" Priscilla asked the moment the door was opened to her knock. "What have you done? Mama is in a rare taking. In fact, I have never seen her so angry. She demands your presence immediately."

Madeline feigned a calm she was far from feeling. "I am sure I do not know why our mother should be so upset. Nor can I perceive what I have to do with the matter."

Priscilla's expression went from concern to skepticism, her lovely eyebrows lifting like a bird's wings. "Coming it much too brown, Maddy."

"I do not know wh—"

"Gammon. Allow me to inform you that your face betrays you. You resemble the cat who dined upon his master's songbird."

Madeline summoned a teasing smile for her sister's benefit. "Never tell me I have yellow feathers clinging to my whiskers."

Priscilla shook her head. "Not yellow. Blue. And not feathers. It is your cloak that bears witness against you. From what I was able to overhear, it *billows* in the wind."

Madeline groaned.

"I knew it! I suspected you were up to something this morning when I saw you wearing your blue jaconet." Priscilla's lake blue eyes fairly danced with curiosity. "Tell me immediately, Maddy. What have you been about, and why did you not take me along?"

"Hush, do, before someone overhears. I must hold my own counsel for the moment."

"But you will tell me later? Please say you will. No one ever tells me anything."

Promising nothing, and leaving her sister agog with conjecture, Madeline squared her shoulders and made her way down to the front parlor where her mother and Bella waited.

The former sat upon a mauve silk settee, her nose lifted as though exposed to an unpleasant aroma, and her mouth pinched with indignation. Her mulberry pelisse was still buttoned up, and the ribbons of her bonnet remained tied beneath her chin.

If Mrs. Wycliff's anger was cold, Bella's was white-hot. The beautiful young matron had tossed her stylish crimson cloak upon a gold slipper chair and now paced the already worn Aubusson carpet, her hazel eyes flashing with fire.

"Well, miss," Mrs. Wycliff began the instant Madeline closed the door behind her. "What have you to say for yourself?"

"How could you?" Bella chimed in, not allowing the

accused to answer their mother's question. "Have you no pride? Are you lost to all sense of what is expected of a Wycliff?"

This last accusation stiffened Madeline's spine as nothing else could have. "I am all too aware of what is expected of *me* as a Wycliff."

Since the sarcasm was lost on her sister, Madeline continued, "As for my pride, I believe I have sufficient. Far too much, in fact, to tolerate being cross-examined by my own sister."

Having said that, Madeline turned and gave her attention to her mother. "Ma'am, I collect that you saw me earlier on the road and wish an explanation."

"There can be none!" interjected Arabella.

"Pray, enlighten me," Mrs. Wycliff said. "How came you to be galloping about the countryside in that exceedingly hoydenish manner? And with a person whose actions, as well as his rough clothes, proclaim him a member of the lower orders."

Madeline took exception to this animadversion and discovered within herself a strong desire to defend Philip against her mama's criticism. However, there was nothing she could say in his defense. He was not of the gentry, and no matter how much she enjoyed being in his company, she could not expect any mother to be pleased to see her daughter a participant in such an unequal association.

"It is a simple story actually," Madeline began. "Comet bolted at a loud noise and ran away, leaving me stranded. I had thought I would be obliged to walk, and had already begun to do so, when by good fortune I encountered Philip, the man on the horse. He saw me safely home. That was all there was to it."

"And who," her indignant sister asked, "is this Philips person?" She spoke the name as though it were a surname, and as such, a proper form of address for a servant. "Did anyone else see you with him?"

Madeline lifted her chin in defiance of Bella's continued inquisition. "I would not care if the entire world had seen me. For my part, I find nothing amiss in accepting safe escort from a gentl—a man—who is known to me. But I suppose the very proper Lady Townsend would have preferred that I spurn his offer and risk being accosted on the road by some vagabond."

Arabella deflected Madeline's barb, posing her next question to Mrs. Wycliff. "Do you see what comes of allowing my sister to run all over the countryside, meddling in the lives of the cottagers? And basket weaving, of all things! So very *déclassé*. As I told you earlier, Mama, her participation in that business is quite unseemly."

Madeline breathed deeply in hopes of calming her rising anger. "I did not know, Bella, that you had been appointed the new arbiter of propriety. May one hope it is a salaried position?"

"Do not be vulgar," advised her sister. "As for propriety, I wonder at your temerity in uttering the word, after riding pommel with a person in his shirtsleeves, your skirts and cloak blowing all about. So disgusting. I, for one, pray that none of our acquaintances witnessed your escapade. Most of all, I hope this day's misadventure may not have ruined all Priscilla's chances."

"Chances for what?" Madeline asked quietly, hoping Bella's anger would lead her into revealing her plan to wed Priscilla to the nabob.

"Her chances of becoming—" But Bella was not so easily led. Recovering, she turned to Mrs. Wycliff, bidding her mother talk some sense into her eldest daughter. "I beg you do it now, Mama. Before the family name is trampled in the dust."

"Madeline," Mrs. Wycliff said, "you will oblige me

by conducting yourself in a manner befitting a gentleman's daughter."

"But I—"

"And from this time forward," her mother continued, her voice so cold Madeline felt the chill from across the room, "I insist that you eschew the company of inferiors."

In contrast to Madeline's disagreeable reception at Wybourne, Philip's return to Balenger Hall was made jolly by the arrival of Mr. Quintin Devon, a young gentleman whose older brother had been Philip's best friend at Eton. In those years before Philip's father took him out of school and set sail for the ill-fated *new beginning* in India, the two schoolboys had been inseparable.

Espying the visitor tooling his maroon and yellow Stanhope up the driveway, Philip gave the gelding his head and sped across the park to meet the unexpected guest just as he pulled up before the portico.

"Quint," he said when both horses were reined in. "What brings you to Somerset? Nothing amiss with Lord Holmes, I trust."

"No, sir. My father is in excellent health. It is just . . ."

Philip studied the young gentleman whose athletic build and handsome face were so like that of his older brother, Harry. The shy smile, too, was like Harry's, and for a moment Philip could almost believe his old friend was before him.

But he was not. Harry was gone now, like so many of England's best and brightest, killed at Waterloo.

Quintin Devon, still three months short of his majority, was now his father's heir, and Philip knew the unlooked-for responsibility weighed heavily on the lad. "Never mind what it is just, stripling. Whichever of the fates has sent you to me, I offer my thanks, for I am heartily sick of my own company."

"Sir, it is I who should thank you, for not being vexed at my unannounced arrival. After all, you will hardly be wanting a visit from a person you cannot have known existed four months ago."

Philip glanced at the sleeve of the young man's single-cape driving coat, where the pinholes still gave evidence of the recently discarded mourning band. "Harry Devon's brother will always be welcome with me," he said, "be he new friend or old."

Leaning forward, Philip offered the visitor his hand in greeting.

"Thank you, sir."

"Best save your thanks until after you have seen the inside of my home. For I should be surprised if you have ever been a guest in a more ramshackle or run-down establishment. You might well be raining curses down upon my head once you see the chamber in which you will be expected to sleep."

The young man smiled again, only this time his brown eyes reflected their willingness to observe life's sunny hours. "I believe Harry had the right of it, for he was used to say that you were a great jokester."

"Nay, lad. I am in earnest. Upon first entering the best of the guest chambers, I mistook the bed hangings for gossamer silk. You may imagine my dismay when, upon closer examination, I discovered the bed to be draped in years—nay, tens of years—of spiderwebs. But," he added offhandedly, "I suppose a fine gentleman such as yourself is too well-mannered to take exception to a few thousand spiders crawling about his face in the dark of night."

"Sir!" the young man said, his smile even more in evidence. "You are the most complete hand."

Philip crossed his heart. "Word of a Balenger."

"That is as may be, sir, but if Singh is with you, I doubt he has allowed even one such creature to remain within doors."

"Be it on your head, then," Philip added. "And never say I did not warn you."

A quarter of an hour later, forewarned but undeterred, Mr. Devon allowed himself to be shown to the red bed-chamber, a room which, although no longer in the first style of elegance, was at least clean and free of wildlife.

"Since you have not brought your man," Philip said, "shall I send Singh up to unpack for you?"

"No, sir. I can manage on my own. Besides," he added, pointing to the single valise he had set beside a bed innocent of hangings—man-made or otherwise, "I have traveled light." He ran his fingers through his short cropped brown hair. "I was not all that certain of my welcome."

Noting the young man's uneasiness, Philip spoke quietly. "But you came anyway. Pluck up to the backbone; just like your brother."

Mr. Devon shook his head. "I have not Harry's fear-lessness—nor his dash. Although I always wanted to be like him. What I did not want was to be the future Baron Holmes."

"Of course you did not." Philip laid his hand on the young man's shoulder. "No one believes that of you, just as no one expects you to step right into Harry's shoes. Least of all Lord Holmes. Nevertheless, when I visited Stavely, I could see that your father was eager for you to learn how to administer your future holdings. Is that what has sent you to my humble abode? A surfeit of learning?"

"That . . . and a rather foolish fancy."

Quintin Devon moved away, as if desirous of seeing

the view from the bedroom window. When he spoke again, his voice was stiff with embarrassment. "I miss Harry. You cannot know how much."

"Perhaps not. One thing I know without question, however, that your brother was a man worthy of our remembrance."

"Thank you," he said quietly. "He was used to tell me some of the rigs you and he got up to while you were at school, what friends you were. I suppose it was no wonder that when you came to pay your respects to Father, I felt almost as if some of Harry had come with you. I . . . I think I came here in hopes of finding a little more of my big brother."

"Harry is not here, lad. I wish he were."

Philip observed the visitor. Such a serious young man, and one who had been too long in the company of a grieving parent. He needed to rejoin the world. To be young again. To frolic and take part in the happy, foolish activities of youth.

While pondering the problem, Philip walked to the door, stopping just inside the threshold. "Your brother was a great one for taking charge. During our first year at Eton, he and I came to cuffs over that matter more than once. If it would make you feel more at home, I could boss you around like old Harry would have done."

Quint turned from the window, his brown eyes wide with surprise. "Sir?"

"My first order: See you do not keep me waiting for my supper. We dine at six."

"No, sir. I would never—"

"My second order: No more of that *sir* business. It is Philip."

"Yes, sir—I mean, Philip."

"This one last thing is most important, see you never

forget it. When we go fishing, *I* catch the biggest fish. Understood?"

A large grin spread across the handsome young face, revealing strong white teeth. "Harry was right! You are the most—"

"Perfect host? Please, lad, you put me to the blush."

Philip stepped out of the room and closed the door upon the visitor's laughter.

That evening, the two gentlemen at Balenger Hall occupied themselves with selecting their fly-fishing gear for the morrow. Comfortably situated in the wainscoted game room, Philip and his guest ignored the numerous moth-eaten animal heads adorning the walls and gave their attention to examining the long-forgotten stash of equipment.

After choosing rods of suitable length and flexibility, they returned to their comfortable red leather chairs, which were situated on either side of a slate hearth where a fire burned cozily. Taking care not to get too near the flames, the gentlemen gave their reels a thorough cleaning with oil-soaked rags. Later they removed the line from its dry storage box, then wound it onto the reel. Lastly they perused the box for hooks whose points were sharp, unbent, and free of rust.

While the fishermen beguiled the evening discussing the relative merits of their sporting paraphernalia, two miles away at Wybourne Madeline paced the floor of her bedchamber, her thoughts in total discord.

Eschew the company of inferiors. A member of the lower orders. Her mother's words fastened themselves upon Madeline's brain like barnacles upon the hull of a ship, and she could think of no way to wrest them free.

The words were true, of course. Even though Philip

had called himself a buccaneer—a description capable of rekindling Madeline's girlhood fantasies—in the real world, an ordinary seaman was a member of the lower orders. A hopelessly ineligible *parti*.

Yet there was between Philip and Madeline an undeniable affinity of souls. Almost from the moment they had met, she had known that within Philip dwelled a spirit capable of understanding the spirit that lived inside her.

She was drawn to him. In his company she felt happy. More alive than she had ever been. Womanly. Imbued with a woman's courage to admit her admiration of his manliness, as well as her pleasure at his obvious appreciation of her femininity.

But such feelings had nothing to do with ladies and gentlemen! Nothing to do with gentry and laborer. They were appropriate only to a man and a woman unencumbered with family. Unfettered by social restrictions.

Madeline had lived her entire life within the bounds of those restrictions. Even though she often felt very nearly suffocated by the constraints imposed upon her, she had no wish to alienate herself from her family, or from her friends. Nor, at five and twenty, was she in imminent danger of trying to make a conquest of Philip, or of attaching him to herself in any permanent way. Doing something of that nature was completely out of the question.

But eschewing his company—never seeing him again—that notion cut up her peace more than she had thought possible.

Throughout most of that sleepless night, Madeline relived the conversations she had enjoyed with Philip, as well as the one she had not enjoyed with her mother. After all the arguments had been weighed, and all the reasons for ignoring those arguments had been enumerated, Madeline was no closer to solving the dilemma than she had been earlier in the evening when she claimed the headache and locked herself in her room.

How could she pretend that Philip did not exist? Or seeing him, how could she nod politely and pass on by without a word?

By daybreak she had the headache in earnest.

Hoping that fresh air might soothe her throbbing temples, she dressed quickly, threw her cloak around her shoulders, then tiptoed down the steps and out the front door.

The sun had not yet dispelled the morning fog, and the air that brushed Madeline's face was cool and moist. She breathed deeply, letting the freshness clear her head. As she strolled along the pebbled carriageway toward the entrance to the estate, her boots made little noise, the sound muffled by the woolly clouds that hovered mere inches above the ground.

In the distance, trees and hedges were obscured, making it difficult to differentiate between flora and fauna. Had it not been so, Madeline would have seen the young gypsy boy before he stepped onto the path in front of her, startling her into uttering a gasp.

The lad was quite small, otherwise she might have screamed at his sudden appearance. Big obsidian eyes overpowered the boy's thin face. His coat and breeches hung loosely on his undersize frame, the clothes appearing older than he was and twice as dirty.

"Morning, missus," he said. "Be you Lady Townsend?"

Madeline had meant to inform him that she was Lady Townsend's sister, but she got only as far as, "I am—"

"Been waiting for yer ladyship this hour and more, I have. Some mort give me a half crown to bring you a message."

Assuming the youngster had brought a letter from her

sister's husband, Madeline held out her hand. "You may give it to me."

The youngster jumped back as if afraid she meant to grab him; then he tapped his finger against the side of his head. "The words be in my nous box. But I can tell 'em right and tight."

Lowering his voice, he said, "The mort wants the money what's owed him. He says you got three days to get it to him. If he ain't got his gelt by then, he says to tell you, you'll be sorry."

Madeline stared, unable to believe the words she had just heard. This was no billet-doux from husband to wife. Like the boy, she lowered her voice. "What did the—uh—mort mean by, 'You'll be sorry'?"

To demonstrate, the boy dragged his grimy finger across his throat. At the same time he made a sound out of the corner of his mouth that, if it were not an accurate imitation of a gullet being slit, it was close enough to send shivers down Madeline's spine.

"Nasty-looking bloke, he was, if you get my meaning. Wouldn't take no chances if I was you, missus. Best give him his money."

Chapter 5

Having delivered his message, the boy turned and ran away, vanishing into the enveloping grayness as quickly as he had appeared.

"Wait!" Madeline called after him. "Where is the man who gave you the message? Is he close by? When did he . . ."

There was no point in continuing. The only sound she heard was that of her own voice, and it was quickly absorbed by the fog, leaving only an eerie, silent void. Suddenly feeling alone and vulnerable, she turned and ran back to the house, as though pursued by the nasty mort who had sent the threatening message.

Once inside the foyer, Madeline bolted the heavy wooden door and leaned against it, her breathing ragged, her hands shaking.

Three days. It might as well be three minutes, for Bella had no way of obtaining fifteen thousand pounds in that time. And when her sister failed to pay the mort, he would come to Wybourne, where the only man on the place was Jem, the coachman.

As Madeline slowly climbed the stairs, her knees so weak she was obliged to coax her limbs into taking each new step, she passed through her mind all the possible avenues of help. Of course, her father might be home within the allotted time; in which case, he could handle the situation. Except that one never knew how long Papa would be gone to one of his race meets. He could return today, or he could just as easily stay away for a fortnight.

Unfortunately anything later than three days, and Papa might return to find his loved ones murdered in their beds. Madeline shuddered at the memory of the young gypsy boy drawing his finger across his throat.

One possibility occurred to her. She could send word to Squire Sandingham. He was the justice of the peace; it was his duty to rid the neighborhood of criminals. It mattered not that the type of miscreants with whom the squire usually dealt were villagers who had imbibed too much at the local pub. Still he was the proper person to contact about this threat.

Fast on the heels of that thought, Madeline recalled the squire's gout and his nearly eighteen stone of corseted girth. Philip had the right of it the other day when she had warned him about poaching. He had said the local squire would give him no cause for alarm, not after the kind of brigands he had known.

Madeline stopped, her foot on the top stair. Philip! Of course. She must be all about in her head; otherwise she would have thought of him immediately. Philip knew how to deal with such men.

By the time she reached her bedchamber, Madeline's heart had slowed to its normal pace. Philip. Yes. He would know what to do.

She would go to him. As soon the sun burned away the fog, she would go through the wood to the brook. Perhaps she would find Philip there. If necessary, she would go all the way to the Hall. And if she had to confront that turbaned giant who guarded the door, she would do that, too.

"Surely you are roasting me," Mr. Quintin Devon said. "Are you telling me that none of your neighbors know you are here?" With his fly rod resting in the crook of his arm, he followed Philip into the water, albeit reluctantly. Unlike his host, he did not wade out toward the very center of the brook, reticent to chance having the chilly water overrun the tops of his boots. For the same reason, he chose to stand in the soft sand rather than risk a position atop one of the slippery rocks visible just below the water's surface. Stopped at what he hoped was a choice spot, he said, "I cannot credit that no one knows you are here, especially since news of the nabob's arrival in London spread over town like snow in February. How have you kept your presence a secret?"

Before replying, Philip positioned his thumb along the top of the rod for a true feel. Satisfied, he waved his arm backward then forward sending his line whirring through the air. The colorful fly landed near a submerged boulder, where he let it drift for several moments before casting it at a likelier spot farther down the stream. "So far," he replied, "Singh has managed to turn all callers away from the door. All, that is, save one."

"And why was he not denied?"

Philip hesitated a moment before answering. "Not he. She."

Quint busied himself with his reel. "I see," he said softly.

"No. You do not see."

Philip was much inclined to say no more upon the subject, not wishing to discuss Madeline with anyone, but after giving the matter some thought, he decided her reputation would be in less danger if he explained the whole.

"I met the lady—and mark me, she is most definitely a lady—quite by accident. Her father's lands begin there on the opposite bank, and I startled her, causing her to fall into the brook."

"And the lady has not informed one and all that the nabob is in residence? A most unusual female, to be sure, to keep to herself such an interesting bit of news."

Philip tried his luck at a spot near the bank where fallen limbs and leaves made a perfect hiding place for the elusive trout. "She does not know."

"Does not know what?"

"That I am the nabob."

Surprised, his companion took an ill-advised step, slipped, and was forced to drop his fly rod in order to save himself a dunking. After regaining his balance, he pushed the sleeve of his jacket and his shirt up, then reached into the water to retrieve the rod.

"*Brr,*" he said, shaking the droplets from his arm before hurriedly rolling the sleeves back down. "I do not wonder that the lady is unaware of your identity. After falling into this icy rivulet, most likely she contracted pneumonia, went straight to her bed, and is even now out of her head, tossing and turning in fevered delirium."

"Not she. I assure you, Miss Wycliff is made of sterner stuff."

"Is she, now? How interesting."

Philip's thoughts returned to Madeline as she had looked when he pulled her out of the water and up onto the bank. He remembered the way her wet hair hung about her shoulders and how her dress clung provocatively to her lovely curves. He felt the corners of his mouth pull into a smile. "Actually, she is a lady with a very romantic turn of mind, and she saw the entire episode as an adventure."

"She sounds like a real trump. But that still does not explain how you managed to keep your identity from her."

"Actually, I had nothing to do with it. She mistook me for a workman of some kind, employed by the nabob, and at that moment, I found the assumption suited my wishes for anonymity."

"At that moment? Am I to infer that it does not suit your wishes now?"

"You have the right of it. Yesterday, when we—"

"Oh, ho. So you have seen the lady a second time."

"I have."

"Surely you did not allow her to continue in the belief that you are a workman?"

Quint's tone held a hint of censure, and Philip felt impelled to explain himself—a thing he did not often do. "In that instance, she came upon *me* by surprise. I had not expected to see her so soon again. If our second meeting had been under formal circumstances, I would have requested that someone introduce us. Then, I think we might have been able to laugh away the misunderstanding at the brook."

"But not now?"

"Now, I fear I have left it too long. The first time she might have forgiven as a jest. The second time, however . . ."

"She may not find amusing," Quint supplied helpfully.

"Just so," Philip replied, wishing he could disagree with the assessment. "She has spoken candidly of herself, her family. We have even discussed the nabob. I am afraid there is no way of informing her of my true identity without causing her embarrassment. Or worse yet, incurring her anger."

"And that would bother you?"

This time Philip decided he had said all he wished to upon the subject—much more than he had meant to. He left the question unanswered, concentrating his attention upon a hard-shell water bug that jumped from a clump of fetid leaves to land midstream, making endless ripples in the water.

When the final ripple ran its course and disappeared, as though it had never been, Philip waded five or six meters farther downstream, putting some distance between himself and his visitor. It was only when he heard Quint speak again that he turned to look at the young man.

"What did you say? I could not hear—"

"Careful of your footing, ma'am," Quint said as he offered Madeline his hand to assist her while she stepped across the stones to the Balenger side of the brook. "I must warn you that this water is devilish cold. If you should fall in, you . . ."

As though suddenly guessing to whom he was speaking, the young man glanced quickly in Philip's direction, his eyes beseeching his host to come to his rescue before he uttered something imprudent.

Philip obeyed the silent summons, slogging his way through the water and up onto the fern-covered bank. One look at Madeline's face was enough to tell him that she had come on an errand of some importance.

After leaning the fly rod against the base of a greenwood tree whose roots were almost totally exposed by years of water lapping against the bank, he hurried up to where Madeline stood, her cloak wrapped around her as though to protect her from something other than the chill in the air. "What is amiss?"

"I . . ." She looked toward the water and Quint, who was making a gallant effort to be inconspicuous. "I should not have come."

When she turned to move away, Philip laid his hand upon her shoulder. "Do not go. 'Tis but a young friend of the Balenger's, come to rusticate a few days. He has only just put off mourning for his brother and is in need of some recreation."

"Of course. I should not have intruded."

"You are speaking fustian, lass. You could never intrude. Come, allow me to present him to you." Raising his voice, he called, "Mr. Quintin Devon, of Stavely, I make you known to Miss Wycliff, of Wybourne."

Quint made a creditable bow, considering his precarious footing. "Your servant, ma'am."

"How do you do, Mr. Devon. I hope the fish are cooperating this morning."

"With one another, perhaps, ma'am. As far as succumbing to my lure, they seem, rather, to be conspiring against me."

— Madeline smiled that lovely, honest smile, the one that seemed equipped with a homing device that allowed it to travel a direct route to Philip's solar plexus.

"You might try over here," she said, "near this valiant old greenwood. I have often seen rather large specimens swimming beneath the tree's exposed roots."

"Or try farther downstream," Philip suggested, giving the young man a jerk of his head for good measure.

"Good idea," Quint responded, stepping away as he spoke. "I will try my luck in that spot Philip deserted."

As soon as they were alone, Philip took one of Madeline's hands and held it between both of his. "Now, tell me what has upset you."

The instant he took her hand, his strong, warm fingers sent reassuring messages up Madeline's arm to her brain. Any lingering doubts she may have had regarding the advisability of coming to him were dispelled when she looked up into his gray eyes. She had done the right thing. Calmness permeated her soul.

"This morning," she began, "a young gypsy boy gave me a message meant for my sister."

As clearly and succinctly as possible, she told Philip the entire story. At its conclusion, she said, "I am out of all sympathy with Bella and Lord Townsend for laying this problem at our doorstep, but as you will have surmised, it is much too late for casting blame. Further-more, it will serve no purpose. What I need now is sound advice."

"I could lend you the fifteen thousand," he said quietly.

"An excellent suggestion. And while we are speaking of miracles, I should like to be blessed with blond curls. Also, I have always wanted a pleasant singing voice. For you must know, I have absolutely no ear for music and—"

"You," he said, his voice warm and caressing, "are a constant source of delight."

"Do be serious," she bade him.

Taking his reprimand in good part, Philip squeezed her hand, smiling at her with such genuine warmth that Madeline very nearly forgot her troubles.

"You have three days' grace," he said. "If you will be guided by me, I advise you to lay this dilemma back in your sister's lap, where it belongs, then go on with your usual activities. If your father has not returned by the reckoning day, I shall take it upon myself to contact Squire Sandingham. Should all else fail, rest assured in the fact that Mr. Devon and I will then arm ourselves and take up residence outside your front door.

"In the meantime," he continued, "if you should observe anyone hanging about the estate, you need only send me word. I know all too well how to deal with such knaves."

Madeline could think of no words adequate to thank him. "I shall do as you advise" was all she said.

Apparently deeming her response sufficient, Philip took her arm and began walking her back toward the stepping-stones. "Now, if you would oblige me, I have a favor to ask of you."

"Anything," she said, stopping just at the water's edge.

A devilish gleam lit his eyes. "Nay, lass. When dealing with a buccaneer, you must never offer him carte blanche. The rogue might ask for something you had no notion of offering."

"Such as?" she said a trifle breathlessly.

His gaze held hers. "He might so forget himself as to take you in his arms and seek the answer to a question that has been plaguing him since he first fished you out of the water."

"What?" The word was little better than a whisper.

Philip lifted his right hand and touched his thumb to the corner of her mouth. Then very slowly, very gently, he traced the edge of her bottom lip from one corner to the other. "I wondered," he said softly, "if a mermaid's lips were cool like the sea, or warm like the sunlight."

Hypnotized by his scorching touch, Madeline thought there was every possibility that the mermaid's lips might well be on fire. "Philip. I—"

"Yahoo!" screamed Mr. Devon, startling Madeline so badly that she jumped back from Philip's supporting hand.

"I have caught one! Philip. Miss Wycliff. Come look at him fight. I vow he must be the whale who swallowed Jonah!"

Summoned, the buccaneer and the mermaid followed the bank until they were close enough to watch the visitor play his fish.

The brown trout was by no means a whale, but it weighed at least a stone and fought as fiercely as any denizen of the sea, thrashing about and splashing water several feet into the air. While the spectators called their encouragement to Mr. Devon, he reeled in the line, then let it slack, repeating the strategy numerous times until the fish began to tire.

"He is almost defeated," the sportsman declared. "Bring me the net, please, Philip. I want to take this fellow ashore where I can have a good look at him."

The fish's capitulation needed only another minute. Then, once the victor and the vanquished were on dry land, the trout had to be admired from every angle.

"I want to measure him," Mr. Devon said. "Then perhaps I will buy myself a journal of some sort and record the particulars."

"Better not," Philip replied dryly. "You will not wish positive proof against you when his size grows with each telling."

Madeline was hard-pressed to hide her laughter at the young man's disdain. "Mr. Devon," she offered, "I have a suggestion, if you should like it."

"Ma'am, I should be honored by any suggestion *you* have to make. It is all too obvious that Philip is eaten up with jealousy."

With that, she could contain her laughter no longer and was forced to clamp her hand over her mouth. Philip obviously felt no such restraint and, with the wickedest of grins, offered to toss both fish and fisherman back into the water.

"Mr. Devon," Madeline interjected before the young man felt himself obliged to challenge the buccaneer, "perhaps you would like to have a picture by which to remember your prize?"

"By Jove, ma'am, that is a capital idea. Are you acquainted with anyone capable of producing a credible likeness?"

"You would do better," Philip suggested, "to ask if the artist is quick. Fish have a way of turning on a fellow within a very few hours."

"Ignore him, Mr. Devon, for I think you have the right of it—Philip is a Philistine. And before he threatens me with a dampening, I—"

"I never would," Philip declared, though the smile lurking behind his eyes gave Madeline cause to doubt his sincerity.

"As I was saying, sir, before I was so rudely interrupted, I fancy I could capture a likeness you would not find contemptible."

"You, ma'am? By Jove. That is good of you." Then, as if suddenly remembering his manners, "But only if it would not be too much of a bother."

Madeline smiled at the young man. "It would be my pleasure, Mr. Devon."

She inspected the fish once again, this time noting fin and color with an artist's eye. "I think I know how it should be done, sir. Have you, perhaps, a nicer creel than this one? One that would contrast with the color of the trout and show your prize to best advantage?"

Looking at the woven basket lying at his feet, its yellow sides dulled and cracked with age, the young man shook his head.

"It is of no consequence," Madeline said, "for I know just the place to purchase one. If you should wish to present yourself at Wybourne within the hour, along with your fish, I will drive you to a place where you may choose from a number of very fine creels."

"Please, ma'am, allow me to drive you. I think you will find my gig quite comfortable."

"As you will, Mr. Devon. I shall return to my home and wait for you there."

Philip would not hear of Madeline walking back through the woods alone, so he accompanied her to within sight of the kitchen door. They had spoken little during the walk, and now Madeline remembered that earlier he had wanted to ask a favor of her. "What may I do for you?" she asked.

Taken by surprise, Philip remained quiet, while any number of fascinating possibilities leapt to his mind—all of which were better left unvoiced.

"You bespoke a favor," she reminded him.

Recovering his composure, he said, "I wished merely to suggest that, for the next three days, you not drive out alone."

"A sensible suggestion," she replied, "and one I shall certainly heed. Thank you for your concern."

He said nothing more, only watched until she was safely inside the house. While he walked back to the brook, then continued to the hall, Philip wondered if Madeline would still be thanking him if she knew how close she had come to being swept into his arms and soundly kissed.

He smiled. Somehow, he could not convince himself that she would be too angry to forgive him for the kiss. No Bath miss, she was a lady with a lot of pluck. Had she not already shown a marked degree of tolerance in the face of his numerous impertinences?

And now, as he passed beneath the portico, entered through the heavy front door, then bound up the steps of the carved oak staircase two at a time, he composed in his head a letter he hoped Madeline would never discover. The letter was not only an impertinence but also an invasion of her privacy.

He meant to contact Sir John Fielding's Bow Street Runners to request they send a couple of detectives to Little Easton, Somerset. One "red breast" to investigate the source of the threat that had frightened Madeline, the other to guard her against harm.

Chapter 6

"I was quite happy to leave the Hall," Mr. Devon informed Madeline as soon as they were out on the road, his prettily behaved sorrel mare pulling the Stanhope at a crisp trot. "The nabob's new bailiff arrived this morning, and word must have been borne upon the wind that the man would be interviewing and hiring laborers. The place is a veritable madhouse, with workmen of all kinds queuing up before the side entrance."

"That is wonderful news," Madeline said, "for employment is sorely needed in Little Easton, as it is needed everywhere. It is a sad reality that difficult times visit the poor first and quit them last."

"That is true. Happily, Ph—what I mean to say is— the nabob has in mind to employ several dozen people. He means to introduce a number of improvements to the house and to his lands."

"Many of the cottages are in sad repair as well," Madeline informed him. "I hope the nabob has plans for those."

"I believe he does, ma'am, for there were thatchers and masons among the queue, identifiable by the tools of their trade prominently displayed about their persons.

"As for the farms," he continued, "the nabob hopes to see those manned and in production as quickly as possible, and has been reading up on all the latest farming methods.

You know, improved strains of cattle and seed, crop rotations, drainage. That sort of thing. Also, Singh has hired a corps of women from the village to clean the Hall from top to bottom."

Casting a sideways glance at his passenger, he said, "Of course, what the Hall really needs is a woman's touch."

"I assure you, sir, that if the mamas of Somerset have anything to say to the matter, a wife is even now awaiting the nabob's arrival."

After voicing that unbecoming piece of old-cattishness, Madeline had the grace to blush, remembering too late that her youngest sister numbered among the prospective candidates.

Fortunately for her composure, Mr. Devon seemed more interested in his horse than her comment. Spying a relatively smooth stretch of road, he encouraged the sorrel to a gallop, and in no time the stylish maroon and yellow Stanhope was eating up the five miles to Little Easton.

As the gig moved along at its fast clip, Madeline's attention was fixed upon keeping the ostrich feathers, which adorned her cream and gold cornet bonnet, out of her mouth. Therefore, she was surprised when her companion asked her if she had any recollection of the nabob's grandfather.

"Mr. Horace Balenger? I do not recall ever having seen him, for you must know, in his later years he was a confirmed recluse. But I have heard stories of him. None of them flattering, I might add."

"They would not be," her companion agreed. "According to my brother, Harry, the old miser begrudged every groat he had to spend on his son. And as for his grandson, the old man never saw him above once."

"Unconscionable. How can a man simply ignore his grandchild?"

"Sent for him that one time, when the lad was about ten or so. I suppose the old goat wanted to see if he could mold the boy into his own image. From what I hear, the visit was not a success. The boy adored his father and would hear nothing disparaging about him, even from his grandfather. The story is, old Balenger sent the lad back to school in less than a sennight."

"Poor little boy. How sad to know he was not wanted. Such knowledge leaves its imprint upon a child. Small wonder he did not return to his grandfather following his father's death."

The travelers remained silent for a time, and after a space of quiet Madeline apologized again for not inviting Mr. Devon into the house when he arrived. "For my mother and both my sisters were from home."

"I quite understand, ma'am. Please, think nothing more of it."

"You are very kind, sir. If my family have not returned by the time we have purchased the creel and are ready to begin the drawing, I shall bring the easel outside so that you may observe my progress. Meanwhile, you may turn left at the next break in the hedgerow. The fifth cottage is our destination."

After slowing the mare to a walk, Mr. Devon turned onto a small, rutted track. On either side of the track, at varying intervals, stood cottages of different ages and styles, all of them built of the local yellow stones and roofed with thatch.

In the front gardens of the respective cottages, Mr. Devon spied women and older-aged children sitting upon three-legged stools, everyone busily employed at a task the gentleman had never seen before.

"What on earth are those cottagers doing?" he asked.

"They are preparing the rods for the basket weavers."

Mr. Devon observed the workers, fascinated by what he saw. On the ground, within easy reach of the low stools, were small mounds of straight, slender sticks. Each of the workers held a device composed of two iron bars that were joined together at one end. From the mound they selected a rod that they passed through first one end of the tool and then the other. Their movements were surprisingly swift, the motion producing a high-pitched, whipping sound.

As he and Madeline continued on their way, she waved her hand, acknowledging the many greetings she received from the workers they passed. "Each cottager rents a planting bed from one of the local farmers," she said, "and in those beds they grow their osiers. The rods you see are cut from those osiers."

"And that fork-looking tool they are using, what is that?"

"It is called a brake. They peel only the rods that are to be used for white baskets. The others are prepared by boiling."

Pointing to the cottage they were approaching on the right, Madeline said, "That is our destination. It is the home of Willem Frome, the finest basket weaver in the village. You will not find his equal anywhere in Somerset. Possibly not in the entire country."

Mr. Devon halted his gig before an old wattle and daub cottage that had been built to follow the contours of the ground, its shape almost round. Having many such irregular-shaped cottages on his own lands, he knew it had, in all likelihood, housed two centuries' worth of dwellers, little having been altered in that time save an occasional rethatching of the hipped roof.

"Good day to ye, Miss Wycliff," greeted the wizened little old man who sat on the ground to the side of the cottage. With his thick smock tucked securely into the waist of his rough trousers and his legs spread out before him, the weaver held a lapboard between his knees. Arranged about him, yet close at hand, were his knives, bodkins, and sundry other tools.

"Good day to you, Willem. I have brought Mr. Devon to see you, for he desires a creel of a particular size and shape. One that will complement the rather impressive brown trout he caught today at Balenger Hall."

"Be ye fixing to render it on paper, miss?"

At Madeline's nod, the old man set aside his lapboard, then rose and invited Mr. Devon to step inside the cottage. "There be one in t'corner t'would do ye well, sir."

Within the half hour, a white creel with maroon-dyed leather trim had been selected and paid for, and the Stanhope was back on the lane, heading toward Wybourne. Both driver and artist were pleased with the purchase.

"I never would have dreamed it," Mr. Devon said, "so many baskets. They fill nearly the entire cottage. The old man has hardly any space left for sitting or eating."

"Willem takes his meals with his son, Abel, and Abel's wife, who live in the cottage across the way. So you see, he can afford to use his own space for his baskets."

"But so many. A person could never use half the number the old weaver has for sale."

"I hope you may be wrong, sir, for it is our intention on Saturday to send every last one of Willem's baskets to Bristol. His and those of two dozen other cottagers."

"By Jove," the young man said. "Bristol, you say?"

"Yes. We are gradually building up a good business in that port for fish kiddles, eel traps, and lobster pots, but we hope soon to expand our market to cities other than Bristol. Perhaps as far away as the Continent, or America. We hope to export all types of baskets. Spelks for coaling ships, turnip or chaff baskets for farmers, as well as shopping and fruit baskets for housewives. We can supply them all."

"By Jove," he said again. "Philip said you were a lady with a romantic turn of mind. I think he mistook the matter. I believe you are a lady with a mind for business."

"Oh, no," she replied, as much embarrassed by the first assessment as by the second. "I assure you, I merely offer my assistance to the cottagers, who are but trying to feed their families. I write letters of inquiry for them to prospective buyers, and I sketch pictures of the type of baskets available, so the buyers can see the nature of the wares before placing their orders. In that way the weavers know which baskets to create, and the carters undertake the journey, having loaded their wagons with baskets they know will be purchased. There is no wasted effort."

Mr. Devon would have asked more on the subject, but they reached the entrance to Wybourne and he had to negotiate the turn onto the carriageway, a feat requiring his full concentration. Later, after Jem had come from the stable to take charge of the visitor's horse and gig, basket weaving was the last thing on Mr. Quintin Devon's mind. As he escorted Madeline to the door, that portal was opened by Miss Priscilla Wycliff.

On the instant, all thoughts left Mr. Devon's mind—all save those involving hair the color of spun gold, eyes the clear blue of a mountain lake, and delicately raised eyebrows that reminded him of a pair of birds on the wing.

"Priscilla," Madeline said, "allow me to present Mr. Quintin Devon. Mr. Devon, my youngest sister."

The gentleman seemed to have forgotten those lovely manners which had been in evidence when he was presented to Madeline earlier that day, for he merely stared at her sister, his appearance reminding Madeline of one who has been knocked senseless by an unexpected blow.

Blushing prettily, Priscilla offered him her hand. "Mr. Devon. How do you do?"

"Yes," he said in answer to her question.

Then, as if giving himself a mental shake, he snatched the curly-brimmed beaver from his head and took the young lady's hand, lifting her fingers to within an inch of his lips, the proper distance for saluting a female newly met. "Your servant, Miss Priscilla."

Never slow to grasp a situation—and this one looked quite promising—Madeline said, "Well met, Priscilla, for I have need of you."

Priscilla managed to turn her gaze from the handsome countenance before her. Her shy smile was a perfect testimony to her reaction to the gentleman, for to Madeline's certain knowledge, not once within the young lady's seventeen years had she ever shown the slightest shyness toward anyone, be he prince or pauper.

"Need?" the lady asked.

Hiding her smile, Madeline said, "I have promised to make a sketch for Mr. Devon, and I am persuaded he will be bored beyond permission in a very short time. As you know, nothing is so tedious as watching me sketch a basket. Never mind that our guest has caught a quite remarkable trout to set beside that basket."

"Trout," repeated the lady.

"Yes," Madeline answered patiently. "What I wish you to do, if you would be so kind, is to sit with us while I sketch, so Mr. Devon will have someone with whom to converse while I am occupied with such mundane matters as color and perspective."

"Of course," Priscilla said, seeming to break free of

her bemusement, "I shall be pleased to join you both. Shall I ask Jinksie to prepare us a tea tray?"

"A wonderful idea," said her sister.

"Capital," agreed Mr. Devon.

The three of them spent an enjoyable two hours in the parlor that adjoined Madeline's little office, and if Mr. Devon noticed the furniture's shabby appearance or the threadbare carpet, he was too well mannered to reveal the fact. When he declared that he had stayed overlong and should take himself back to Balenger Hall, thereby giving the ladies' ears a rest from his incessant chatter, both his auditors denied any such discomfort and declared themselves well pleased with the conversation.

In fact, the younger of the two ladies went so far as to let it slip that she had rather enjoyed the restful coze at home, since she had to take herself to the village on the morrow in search of ribbons for a new frock.

Much affected by this piece of information, Mr. Devon bethought himself of a question he had wished to ask. "Is there, perhaps, a circulating library in Little Easton? I did not bring any books with me, and the few volumes to be found at the Hall concern themselves with farming or with the preparation and dispensing of tisanes, nostrums, and purges." He wrinkled his aristocratic nose in distaste.

Laughing at his expression, Madeline informed him that the village did, in fact, number among its attractions a small, but eclectic, circulating library. "And I am certain your subscription would be most welcome."

He busied himself with a minute adjustment to the right sleeve of his dark blue coat. "Have you any notion, ma'am, at what hour of the day the establishment is least crowded?" He asked the question of Madeline, but his brown eyes looked to her younger sister for confirmation.

"Oh, I cannot be certain," Madeline declared. "What say you, Priscilla?"

That damsel gave it as her opinion that the best time was around one of the clock.

"One o'clock," repeated Mr. Devon. "I thank you for the information."

He adjusted the coat sleeve once again, and both ladies waited quietly, in expectation of some further comment. When he said nothing, merely exhaled loudly, Priscilla stepped into the breach.

"If we should chance to meet in the village one day, Mr. Devon, perhaps you might wish to be shown the bridge that was once the only connection between Little Easton and Glastonbury. It is of great antiquity and of particular interest to visitors."

A wide smile attested to the young gentleman's love of antiquities. "Capital idea. I shall live in great hopes that we chance upon one another."

Pleased with this avowal, the fellow history lover offered Mr. Devon her hand, which he raised to his lips for the briefest of salutes.

As he was saying his farewells, the gentleman almost forgot the handsome sketch Madeline had finished of his trout, its brown sides and fin picked out in a washed burgundy that pulled the viewer's eye to the maroon of the white creel. When his attention was called to the oversight, he stammered an apology, put the sketch beneath his arm, then took himself to the door.

His last look back was accompanied by a warm smile for Miss Priscilla.

By the time Mr. Devon alighted from his gig at the door of Balenger Hall, the queue of hopeful applicants had disappeared. However, some among the number must have found success, for the groom who came to take charge of his horse and carriage had not been employed in that capacity earlier in the day.

A similar staffing addition was immediately apparent when a tall, pleasant-faced footman opened the door, called Mr. Devon by name, and after offering to take his hat, informed him that Mr. Balenger was in the book room and would be pleased if his guest would join him there.

That the evening meal was considerably more palatable, and the dishes innocent of those exotic spices preferred by Singh, hinted at a kitchen overseen by a cook familiar with good English fare. A flavorful fish soup was removed with a platter of braised partridges; a well-turned mutton accompanied by mint jelly, green peas, and apple fritters was also removed.

After the footman took the cloth from the table, Singh set before the two gentlemen a silver tray piled high with fragrant macaroons and a decanter of not too contemptible port discovered in Horace Balenger's wine cellar.

"So, Quint," Philip began once Singh had withdrawn from the dining room, "tell me more of Miss Priscilla. Divinely fair, I believe you said."

If Mr. Quintin Devon found an appreciative audience in his dinner companion, the same could not be said for Priscilla. Her sister, Lady Townsend, was horrified to discover that a young man had spent the better part of the afternoon visiting her sisters.

"Who is this person?" she asked, the nervousness in her voice not lost upon Madeline. It was not difficult to guess the reason for Bella's unease, for any male would present a threat to her scheme for marrying their young sister to the nabob.

No more than Madeline did Priscilla appreciate being

interrogated by her sister. Before answering the question, she pressed her serviette to her lips, then pointedly laid it upon the mahogany dining table. "Though I fail to see how it could possibly concern you, Bella, the *gentleman's* name is Quintin Devon, and he is a friend of Maddy's."

"Humph," Bella said inelegantly, leaving her family in no doubt as to her opinion regarding the caller. "Considering Madeline's predilection for low company, I take leave to question Mr. Devon's right to be called a gentleman."

The argument that followed this statement was quite heated, and so liberally sprinkled with name-calling and pieces of resurrected disputes from years past, that Mrs. Wycliff finally grew weary of the noise and took refuge in her old friend, palpitations. "My salts," she demanded in a voice loud enough to be heard above the din, "where are my salts?"

When she finally gained the attention of the two combatants, the lady placed her hand upon her bosom and slumped back into the tall chair. "Please," she said, her voice now only slightly stronger than a kitten's mew, "someone help me to my room, for I fear the onset of one of my spells."

"Now see what you have done," Bella accused, rushing to her mother's side and helping her to rise from the chair. As they neared the dining-room door, she cast an angry glance over her shoulder and informed her youngest sister that she would return. "For I have not said all I wish to say to you, young lady."

"Well, you might just as well— Ouch! Madeline, you stomped my—"

"By the way, Bella," Madeline interrupted calmly, removing her foot from Priscilla's toes, "I have been waiting this age for a moment of private conversation with you. You had a message. It came quite early this morning."

Bella turned quickly, her green eyes bright, her alabaster skin aglow with hope. "From Townsend?" she asked breathlessly.

"No. It was not from your husband. Actually, I did not get the name of the sender, for it was delivered by a young boy. But never fear, like the lad, I remember the whole 'right and tight.' "

Having deflected Bella's anger from their youngest sister, Madeline turned a beatific smile upon that maiden. "Meanwhile, Priscilla, I think you should retire to your bed, for you will not want to appear pulled when we visit the village tomorrow."

Detecting a rebellious light in Priscilla's eyes, Madeline continued, "I will wait here in your stead until Bella returns. Anything our sister had planned to say to you, she can say to me." Then, turning once again toward the door, "Do not make me wait too long, Bella, for I think you will find the message is of some importance."

Chapter 7

If Lady Townsend's strictures of the evening before had any effect upon Miss Priscilla Wycliff, that effect was not apparent in the damsel's choice of ensemble for the all-important trip to Little Easton to procure ribbons.

The day being sunny and clement, she was attired in a soft pink frock of Indian muslin, whose bouffant sleeves reached from her gently rounded shoulders to her elbows, and whose high waist complemented her tall, slender form. Around her shoulders she had thrown a Norwich shawl whose knotted fringe was of a similar pink as that of her dress, and upon her flaxen curls rested a chip straw bonnet with pink ribbons that passed over the hat's brim to tie beneath the wearer's chin.

Madeline, upon viewing her sister as she stepped out the front door, had only one thought, that if Mr. Devon was struck senseless yesterday, today he would receive a telling blow.

Working her kid driving gloves onto her hand, she said, "You are in fine looks, little sister. I vow I feel quite the dowd standing next to you."

"Fustian, Maddy. You will never be a dowd, for that quality within you that makes you such a caring person also makes you quite lovely."

Rendered speechless by this unlooked-for tribute, Madeline took the reins from Jem and climbed up into the gig. Both pleased and embarrassed, she straightened the skirt of her lilac frock, gave a twitch to her paisley shawl, then a tug to the Dutch bonnet whose turned-up brim sported a lilac cabbage rose.

Following close behind her sister, Priscilla had only just taken her place on the hard seat, with no opportunity to compose herself, when Comet decided it was time to go. Fortunately the horse employed his usual snail's pace, so no harm befell the passengers.

As they left the carriageway and turned onto the lane, Madeline was hard-pressed not to compare this sluggish travel to the speed she had enjoyed in Mr. Devon's Stanhope. Yet even that pleasant experience paled in comparison to the thrill of riding with Philip upon his winged Pegasus.

Madeline did not speak of the buccaneer, but when Comet plodded his way past Balenger Hall, she could not resist the urge to look toward the gray stone entrance. It did not escape her notice that her sister also managed a subtle glance in the direction of the iron gate. As it happened, neither lady was rewarded with anything more interesting than a glimpse of an empty carriageway much in need of regrading.

"What color are you looking for?" Madeline asked, hoping to fill the next forty-five minutes with something more interesting than the clop, clop of the gelding's hooves.

"Color? I do not understand what—"

"Ribbons, little sister. Remember? We are come upon an errand. You told Mr. Devon that you needed to purchase ribbons."

"Oh, yes," she answered, recollecting the conversation.

Madeline chuckled. "It would behoove you to put a little more believability into your voice. Else I shall be forced to conclude that this need to visit the draper's is all a hum."

Giving her oldest sister a look filled with impudence, the young lady said, "The color is blue."

"Now I know it is a hum, for neither of us has purchased an ell of anything blue within the last year. However, on the chance that someone might question me, what are the new ribbons supposed to match?"

Confounded for only a moment, the youngest Wycliff turned to her sister, an air of having won a contest evident in her smug expression. "They are to match my eyes," she said.

"Saucy baggage. Do try for a little conduct."

"Ho! Conduct is it? You are a fine one to adjure me to mind my manners. I heard the unholy delight you took in telling Bella about that message from the man who wants his money."

"Priscilla! You eavesdropped. Has no one ever told you that eavesdroppers hear only—"

"Ill about themselves," she concluded. "But I did not hear anything at all about myself—ill or otherwise—and I thoroughly enjoyed hearing the *on-dits* about Lord Townsend." She giggled. "And not for anything in the world would I have missed the shriek Bella made when you imitated that deliciously horrid sound to denote the cutting of a throat."

"Yes, but—"

"Besides," Priscilla continued, "how else am I to find out what is going on? If certain people would take me into their confidence, I would not need to listen in at keyholes."

Madeline considered Priscilla's words, concluding that her sister had a right to know the situation, for if Bella was allowed to implement her plan, Priscilla would be the one most directly affected by the debt and its repayment. Furthermore, if the money was not paid in the next three days, everyone in the house would need to be warned of the threat to their safety.

"The matter is not to be taken lightly," Madeline said, "and I should not have baited Bella. Lord Townsend has amassed gaming debts of fifteen thousand pounds, and now the holder of our brother-in-law's vowels wants payment in full. The man is no gentleman, and he has threatened to resort to violence if the money is not forthcoming within the next three days."

Priscilla drew air through her pursed lips, producing a soft whistle. "No wonder Bella took to her bed with a sick headache. 'Tis enough to give anyone the megrims."

Madeline decided that now was as good a time as any to gauge her sister's willingness to immolate herself upon the altar of family duty. As though the thought had only just occurred to her, she asked, "If it were within your power to pay the debt, would you do so?"

"Me? You must be all about in your head. I have in my reticule the sum total of one shilling, two pence, and a farthing."

"But what if you could—say—marry a gentleman of immense wealth, a man who would be willing to pay the debt. Would you do that?"

The young lady needed no time to ponder the question. "When I marry, it will be to suit my heart. Otherwise, I shall not marry at all. As for paying Townsend's gaming debts, believe me, if the fifteen thousand reposed in my reticule this very moment, I would not so much as undraw the string."

Having delivered herself of this pronouncement, the youngest Wycliff revealed what she considered a much better plan for the spending of the hypothetical funds. "If I had fifteen thousand pounds, I would hire a grand traveling coach drawn by four magnificent horses, and I would have the coachman drive you and me to town, where we would be fitted for dozens of frocks and gowns, each one more beautiful than the last. Then, once we were stylishly rigged-out, we would spend what remained of the money on the most lavish come-outs any two ladies ever enjoyed. "

Her question regarding the *mariage de convenance* answered for good, Madeline entered into Priscilla's foolishness, informing her sister that she would not even consider going to London in a coach drawn by fewer than *six* horses. "For you must know, my dear, that it would be disastrous for us to arrive in London looking shabby genteel."

Nothing more was said of their brother-in-law's gaming debts, and the remainder of the drive was enlivened by outrageous plans for their come-outs. Their nonsensical chatter was brought to a conclusion only when the village was within sight.

"We are arrived," Madeline said as they drove past the blacksmith's, the first shop along the single street that bisected Little Easton. "To spare my blushes, please tell me that you mean to make at least a token appearance at the draper's."

Priscilla scanned the dozen or so shops, from the saddler's on her right, all the way to the top of the street. Her search ended at a handsome old half-timbered building that stood in the middle of the road, forcing anyone who wished to travel farther to go around it. The sign suspended over the entrance read: THE GREEN KNIGHT FAMILY HOTEL AND TAVERN. Quite close to the entrance to the hotel, she spied a young gentleman who leaned nonchalantly against the wall, one booted foot crossed over the other.

The gentleman spied the ladies as well, then straightened and began walking hurriedly in their direction.

"Maddy," Priscilla said, her smile producing a charming dimple in her right cheek, "now you may stop at the draper's."

With only the slightest tug on the reins, Comet was encouraged to halt at the small two-story brick building housing both the draper's establishment and that of the village milliner. The cloth dealer's lad rushed from the shop to take charge of the horse, and as the two ladies alighted from the gig, they heard the tap of a gentleman's boots on the cobblestone street.

"Miss Wycliff. Miss Priscilla," Mr. Quintin Devon said, doffing his beaver and bowing politely. "Well met. And may I say what a pleasure it is for a stranger to look upon familiar faces."

Madeline smiled, while Priscilla offered her hand. "Mr. Devon," said the latter, "I see you decided to come to the village today. May one hope you found the circulating library to your taste?"

"Quite," he said. "A most satisfactory place, I assure you. Volumes for every taste."

The fact that the gentleman was in possession of not even one of those eclectic volumes was not lost upon Madeline. Unaccountably pleased by this, she said, "If you would not find it too much of a bore, sir, you could lend us your opinion on the proper shade of blue for my sister's ribbons."

"With the greatest of pleasure, ma'am. I was wondering, though, if you and Miss Priscilla might be so kind as to postpone your shopping for the nonce, and do me the honor of showing me the bridge? I own, I have been wanting to see it since you mentioned it yesterday."

In light of the hopeful looks turned upon her by both young persons, Madeline would not have refused the request even had she been inclined to do so. "The bridge it is," she said.

Without needing to inquire in which direction they should proceed, Mr. Devon offered an arm to each lady and began strolling toward the top of the street. Several of the local women greeted the two sisters, then turned to admire the handsome, splendidly formed stranger who, although by no means a tulip, was stylishly attired.

He wore a well-cut coat of bottle green, complemented by fawn breeches, a gold-striped waistcoat, modest shirt points, a spotless and unpretentious neck cloth, and highly polished top boots—unexceptional dress for a gentleman enjoying the air in a rural setting.

Within a few minutes, the threesome had left both the village and the curious onlookers behind. As they continued their stroll across a gently sloping meadow toward the ancient stone bridge and the fast-moving river it spanned, Mr. Devon tried to persuade his companions to call him by his given name. "For it is the done thing, among the *ton,* for young ladies to do so. Especially if they have known the gentleman in the country."

"Flummery," Priscilla declared. "I collect you are making a May game of us, *Mr. Devon.* Even if such license were deemed acceptable, which I take leave to doubt, it would not apply to two ladies who made your acquaintance only yesterday."

"Especially then," he insisted. "Do you not see how practical it is?"

"Practical? I believe you mean nonsensical." Priscilla smiled to soften her words, and the gesture bestowed upon the gentleman a glimpse of the elusive dimple in her cheek—a kindness he returned with a smile of his own.

Mr. Devon's next remark had something to do with havey-cavey fellows thinking twice about approaching a lady accompanied by a gentleman she called by his first name. If Priscilla made any reply to this tomfoolery, however, Madeline never knew, for she paid scant attention. She was much more interested in the narrow, arced bridge up ahead.

Or more to the point, she was interested in the tall, dark-haired man who stood on the bridge.

With one booted foot propped on the low, yellow stone parapet, his elbow resting on his knee, the man gazed at the icy blue water of the river as it meandered around a small spit of land, then hurried along its uneven path to tumble at length over an expanse of rough boulders.

A stand of century-old yew trees grew on the spit, and beneath the trees, near the water's edge, a quartet of geese waddled among the sodden grasses and ferns, repeatedly dipping their bills into the muddy greenery in search of bugs.

When one of the fowl took exception to the approach of the three humans, stopping its foraging long enough to stretch its long neck and hiss its displeasure, the man on the bridge looked up. Straightening, he smiled, and even at a distance his teeth shone white and strong against his bronzed skin.

Philip. Silently Madeline mouthed his name.

Ever the pirate, he stood with his powerful legs spread wide beneath him, his posture straight and commanding, as though he never doubted his own strength or ability.

Madeline found herself unable to look away from him, although she told herself it was because she was unaccustomed to seeing him wear a neck cloth. The starched folds of the linen emphasized the strong line of his jaw, the determination of his square chin. Over his buckskin breeches he wore a neat, tobacco brown coat, and though the coat was not in the same style of elegance as Mr. Devon's, Madeline could not help but notice how beautifully the cloth hugged his wide shoulders, or how it seemed to reveal rather than hide his muscular arms.

Philip left the bridge, and while he walked toward them, his stride slow and rolling, as though he still trod the deck of a ship, he looked directly at Madeline.

Still unable to look away, Madeline experienced the oddest sensation that his warm gaze actually caressed her face. Her heart thumped so loudly, she marveled that no one commented on the noise.

"Philip," Mr. Devon called in greeting, "only see how Dame Fortune has smiled upon me. A lovely lady on each arm."

"Some fellows have all the luck," Philip answered. "But you must know that chance is a fickle giver, and will not long allow you to remain in that enviable state." He stopped before them. "Since it was I who made you known to Miss Wycliff, what say you to presenting me to Miss Priscilla?"

"You see how it is?" Mr. Devon said, looking into Priscilla's questioning eyes. "Did I not warn you that some havey-cavey sort would try to insinuate himself into our group? Now, here is proof that—"

"How do you do, Miss Priscilla," Philip said, making her a graceful bow. "I understand that I have you to thank for calling this interesting bridge to our attention. I am in your debt."

When Priscilla looked from Mr. Devon to her sister, her uncertain expression revealing her confusion as to how she should respond to this stranger, Madeline stepped into the breach. Extending her hand, she said, "Good afternoon, Philip."

"It is now," he replied.

Bowing, he lifted Madeline's fingers to his lips for a brief moment. Then, still retaining her hand, he deftly turned so that her arm rested quite naturally within the crook of his. "Come," he said, "allow me to show you the best vantage point for determining the flow of the river."

As they stepped ahead of the younger couple, Philip turned to look over his shoulder. "Please enlighten us about the bridge, Miss Priscilla, for I can see from the workmanship and the thickness of the lichen that it is of great antiquity."

"Yes," she said, her voice still slightly puzzled, "it is quite old, Mr. . . ."

"Please," he said, "call me Philip. Your sister does so."

"I . . . Maddy?"

Madeline's mind raced. She felt quite out of her depth, unsure how she should introduce the buccaneer to her sister. Or even *if* she should. After all, their mother had forbidden further communication between her oldest daughter and Philip. She would definitely not want her youngest daughter associating with him.

As for Philip, Madeline did not understand why he was here.

She knew *what* he was doing, of course. Like a big fish swallowing a smaller fish, he had taken Priscilla's little subterfuge about a trip to the draper's and gone her one better, creating an opportunity for the four of them to meet in this secluded place. But why? Was he aiding Mr. Devon—as she was aiding her sister—thinking the two young people should have a chance to further their acquaintance?

"Quint," Madeline said, using the young man's name, in hopes that by so doing she need not explain her use of Philip's, "I am persuaded you must have similar bridges near your home. Stavely, I believe Philip called it. I have traveled little and know only the environs of my own neighborhood. Tell us, if you please, something of your area."

The gentleman was more than happy to comply with her request and immediately began a description of the locale and attractions of his estate, which was situated in Warwickshire, near Stratford-upon-Avon.

"One thing I am certain you would find of interest, ma'am, for it draws many visitors to the area, is a timber-framed farmhouse at Wilcote, near Aston Cantlow. During her childhood, Mary Arden, the mother of Mr. William Shakespeare, lived there."

"How fascinating," Priscilla said. "It must be quite old."

"Yes, quite. The walls have bowed visibly with age."

"Fascinating," she repeated.

Because the gentleman was obliged to raise his voice to include the couple who walked ahead, and also because Priscilla seemed to be the only one of his audience vouchsafing any questions or comments, very soon his words grew more quiet, the conversation narrowing to include only the two young people who still strolled arm in arm.

"Very smoothly done," Philip said, giving Madeline one of those smiles that always made her feel as if he and she were attuned to one another's thoughts. Unfortunately that smile also erased from her consciousness all her mother's strictures against associating with members of the lower orders.

"I am sure I do not know what you mean," she said airily.

"Ah," he said, "I see you are a dissembler as well as a matchmaker."

Madeline felt her face grow warm. "You wrong me. If by *matchmaker* you mean one of those women who cannot see a personable young gentleman without instantly concluding that he must be pining away to meet one of her unmarried friends, then allow me to inform you, I am not of that number."

"Of course you are," he replied.

"Of all—"

"However, before you come all toplofty and give me the cut direct, allow me to tell you that, in this instance, the personable young gentleman is more than happy to pursue the acquaintance. Furthermore, Quint would be a much more desirable *parti* for your sister than the nabob."

Recalled to her sisterly duties, Madeline said, "I had forgotten about the nabob. I wish you will answer me something, Philip."

"You may ask me anything."

"Now that you have seen Priscilla, how beautiful she is, do you still contend that Mr. Balenger would not wish to marry her?"

"Of a surety," he replied. "Not," he continued, "that Miss Priscilla is not beautiful enough to turn any man's head, for she is a rare gem—a diamond, in fact. It is just . . ."

"Just what?"

"Just that she is not quite in the Balenger's style."

"Oh. I see."

Philip looked down at her, his eyebrows raised in question. "Is that all you have to say? Have you no curiosity as to what the Balenger's preferred style might be?"

"None."

"Have a care. You risk giving the matchmakers of Somerset a bad name."

Madeline detected the teasing light in his eyes and was hard-pressed not to smile at him. "I told you, I am not a matchmaker. But I can see that you are desirous of telling me the nabob's preferences. And since we are at the midpoint of the bridge, so that I should not know in which direction to flee if you were to threaten to toss me overboard—"

"I told you, lass. I would never—"

"Yes. Yes. You would never toss me in the water. I own I would be much more comforted by that vow if, when you said it, you did not always have such trouble hiding your smile."

He threw back his head and laughed. " 'Tis your own fault, little mermaid."

"Mine?"

"I would not have the wish to toss you in, if I had not seen with my own eyes just how delectable you appear when soaking wet."

Madeline gasped, pulling her arm from his. "Sir, you are thoroughly rag-mannered."

"Here again, the blame sits solidly atop your head, lass, for you will keep bringing up the subject of water. I was more than willing to discuss the Balenger, but you insisted upon turning my thoughts to that time at the brook when you—"

"The nabob," she interjected quickly. "I find myself positively consumed with curiosity as to his likes and dislikes."

"Understandable," he said.

Reclaiming her hand, he nestled it back within the crook of his arm. "The cobblestones of the bridge make it unwise for a lady to walk alone."

Although that particular lady had safely crossed this bridge hundreds of times, she did not correct Philip's assumption that she needed assistance, choosing rather to enjoy the support of his arm and keep her history to herself.

"The Balenger," Philip began, "is a man who has had the rare privilege of beholding some of the world's most beautiful women."

"How nice for him," Madeline said, the sarcasm earning her an amused glance from her companion.

"Waspish, lass. Very waspish."

Madeline chuckled, then pretended the sound had been a cough.

"Very beautiful women," he continued, "and I believe I may safely say that Miss Priscilla numbers among the fairest of the fair. However, the Balenger's tastes run a little differently."

"You would have me believe he admires homely misses?"

"Nay. Not homely. Just not in the common style."

Interested in spite of herself, Madeline said, "How is that?"

Philip did not answer right away. Instead he looked into her eyes in a way that made Madeline long to inquire what *he* found admirable in a woman.

"The Balenger likes blue eyes," he said. "But not just any ordinary blue. He fancies the kind that sparkle with fire when the lady believes an injustice is being done, yet go all soft and mysterious when she speaks of matters close to her heart."

When he said that last, his voice was hushed, sending shivers down Madeline's spine and making her long to be the possessor of eyes a man might describe with such tenderness. She sighed. Then, afraid he might guess the cause of her sigh, she hurried to say, "And what of the lady's hair? Is the nabob similarly particular about that?"

"Oh, yes. He prefers brown. Only not just any old brown."

"Somehow I doubted as much."

"You were right to do so, lass. The Balenger likes hair that is soft and silky—curls not the least bit necessary—and of a lightish hue, with just a hint of sherry when the sun chances to caress the lady's head."

For some unaccountable reason, Madeline's hand crept up to touch the tendril Priscilla had insisted she let rest against her cheek.

"As for skin," Philip continued, looking at the tendril's resting place, "it should be smooth and soft, and inviting to a man's touch."

He brought his mouth close to Madeline's ear, speaking in a whisper, so that only she could hear. "Shall I tell you of her lips?"

"No! That is, I think we have talked enough of the nabob's likes and dislikes."

Embarrassed that she had revealed just how much his words had affected her, Madeline looked about for something upon which to comment. The rare sunshine gave the yellow stones of the parapet a golden glow, and she was about to comment upon that fact when she noticed something on the ground just beyond the end of the bridge. Beneath a wide chestnut tree whose leafy limbs stretched in every direction, someone had spread a blanket, and on that blanket reposed a basket filled almost to overflowing.

"Maddy, look," Priscilla said, hurrying to come abreast of her sister, "it is a picnic. Mr.—er—Philip has arranged an alfresco nuncheon. Was that not thoughtful of him? Do say we may stay, for I declare I am famished."

Quint added his voice to her plea. "Please say you will join us, Miss Wycliff."

"I . . ."

Noting her sister's hesitation, Priscilla pulled Madeline aside so that she might speak privately with her. "You must not refuse, Maddy. Otherwise you will appear the veriest ingrate. I was not supposed to tell you this, but Philip went early this morning to purchase that basket from Willem Frome. And he did it just to please you."

Chapter 8

"I heard the most amusing story," Priscilla informed her nuncheon companions. "It is about the nabob."

Philip almost choked upon a macaroon he had only just begun to chew. Quint, on the other hand, his long legs stretched before him on the blanket, laughed as though he were in possession of a secret that made tales of the nabob especially amusing.

"Pray let us hear your story, Miss Priscilla. Philip and I are positively fascinated by *on-dits* concerning the nabob."

Madeline noticed that Philip's scowl did not appear to support the young gentleman's statement, but fortunately for her sister's composure, Priscilla was busy wiping her fingers upon her serviette and did not witness his displeasure.

"I had the account," she began, "from Lizzie Sandingham, who is the squire's oldest daughter."

"How very interesting," Quint said. "I was not aware that the nabob was acquainted with any of his neighbors."

"No, he is not. At least, if he is, I have no knowledge of it. In this instance, Lizzie remember meeting him when he was a lad of about ten. She is of a similar age with the nabob, and they were both invited to a party given to celebrate the anniversary of Bertha Ramsbury's birth."

Madeline had just taken a sip of her lemonade, and apparently she made a sour face, for Philip said, "Not sweet enough?"

She set the goblet beside her on the blanket. "The drink is perfect. I was just imagining what a delightful experience it must have been, being at a party for Bertha Ramsbury."

At her sarcasm, Philip raised his eyebrows in question. "I take it you and Miss Ramsbury are not bosom bows."

She shook her head. "Lady Besford, to give her her married name and title, is the granddaughter of an earl. Because of that fact, she was reared to think herself above the vastly inferior company to be had in the neighborhood."

"That is neither here nor there," Priscilla said, calling her listeners back to the subject, "except that it explains why Lizzie Sandingham so enjoyed relating the story."

"Do continue," Quint said.

"According to Lizzie, Bertha had received a tiara for her birthday, and—"

"A tiara!" Madeline said. "For a ten-year-old? Of all the preposterous—"

"Maddy!"

"Sorry." Lifting the goblet to her lips, she took a sip of the lemonade. "Pray go on."

"Anyway, Bertha had got the tiara, so her mother's dresser arranged the birthday girl's long hair into a nest of curls that fit neatly within the curve of the tiara." She glanced at her sister. "And you must admit, Maddy, no matter what you may think of Bertha, she has lovely hair."

"Is it brown?" Philip asked.

Madeline stayed the glass she had just put to her lips.

"Nothing so commonplace," she informed him. "Her hair is black, and lustrous as a raven's wing."

"Never mind," he said airily. "Please excuse the interruption, Miss Priscilla."

"Of course. Now where was I? Oh, yes, Bertha's party. It was held in the garden, near the folly, so the children could play games and run around without harming any of the Ramsbury's priceless furniture. You must know," she informed them, "that the folly was erected in the middle of a small pond."

When Philip glanced at Madeline, a smile lurking in his eyes, she informed him haughtily, "I beg you will note that *I* did not mention the pond."

Continuing her story, Priscilla said, "Bertha had already ruined the affair for the other children by making slighting remarks about the gifts they had brought. Then she further alienated them by going around claiming to be a princess, insisting that she was destined to marry a prince."

"The tiara went to her head," Quint joked, making Priscilla giggle. "But do go on, please. I find I can hardly wait to hear the nabob's part in this story."

"The way Lizzie told it, several of the boys had found toads in the tall grass at the pond's edge, and Master Balenger, who had captured the largest specimen, suggested they have a toad-jumping contest. The idea was greeted with enthusiasm by all the children. All, that is, except for Bertha."

"Oh, ho," Quint said, "here it comes."

Philip, Madeline noticed, had become unusually quiet.

"Bertha ordered Master Balenger to put all the nasty, slimy toads back, and when he went right on drawing off the boundaries for the contest, she grew angry and repeated something unkind she had heard about the boy's father."

"Poor boy," Madeline said.

"Do not waste your sympathy, Maddy, for the poor boy held his own. They were much of an age, so he looked her squarely in the eyes and told her the only way she would ever marry a prince was if she found one trapped in a frog's body. Then, to the delight of the other children, he suggested she start her search by kissing the one he held. With that, he set the toad right in the middle of the tiara, atop Bertha's curls."

It was a toss-up as to who laughed harder, Quint or Madeline. "Priceless," Madeline declared once she had herself under control.

"I wonder," Philip said quietly, "if the little girl sustained any emotional damage as a result of the experience?"

"If she did, it would explain a lot," Madeline suggested, going off into whoops again. "Especially how she could bring herself to wed Lord Besford. For you must know, not only is he a toady of the worst kind, encouraging his wife in her belief in her own consequence, but he is also far from handsome. One can only surmise that Bertha was so frightened by the experience at the party that she lost the ability to tell the difference between a prince and a frog."

With the story told and the nuncheon consumed almost to the last crumb, the two young people grew restless and decided to walk down to the river's edge to see if they could find any violets or heartsease among the ferns. However, judging from the speed with which Priscilla jumped back from the wildflowers, the bees must have believed the pansies under their sole authority.

Without too much evidence of remorse, the young lady and gentleman abandoned their horticultural investigation in favor of a stroll back to the bridge, where they sat upon the parapet and threw rocks and twigs into the rushing water, each one insisting good-naturedly that their *man* would win the race to the rapids.

"Thank you for the nuncheon," Madeline said, busying herself with returning the plates and napkins to the tan basket. "You must have made an impression upon Willem Frome."

"And what makes you think that?"

She lifted the basket, holding it so the sunlight revealed the smooth, snug, flawless craftsmanship. "He sold you one of his best."

From his relaxed position upon the blanket, his back propped comfortably against the base of the chestnut tree and his booted feet crossed at the ankles, Philip admired the basket's workmanship. "If the weaver gave me his best work, I fancy it had less to do with me, and more to do with my having mentioned your name."

Madeline felt her cheeks grow warm. "You told Willem we were friends?"

"I merely told him I had seen the drawing you did for Quint. Why?" he inquired quietly. "Would it embarrass you to acknowledge our friendship?"

"No," she replied.

Deep inside her, Madeline knew she had not spoken with complete honesty. Meeting Philip and having him for a friend was the most exciting thing that had ever happened to her. When she was with him, life was more exhilarating, the most commonplace conversations seemed imbued with charm and wit, and even the simplest picnic food tasted more flavorful. And though all this was true, there were other factors involved. Nothing was ever as sure and certain as one would like it to be.

Philip had lived too long in foreign lands, and as a consequence, he knew little of English life and the social standards to which each level of society adhered. If it were not so, he never would have sought her company;

he would have known that laborers did not form friendships with gentlemen's daughters.

As well, Philip knew nothing of country life. In a village as small and remote as Little Easton, an avowal of friendship was the next best thing to posting the banns and announcing the wedding plans. Also, in the minds of the villagers, if such an avowal was not followed soon by an engagement, it meant someone had been jilted.

For her part, Madeline had no wish to figure as either the jilter or the jilted party, especially not before the people with whom she must spend the rest of her days.

"I am proud to be counted among your friends," she explained, "but you cannot know how quickly news travels in the country. I should not like any friendship of mine to outdistance the nabob's arrival as food for the village gossips."

"Of course," Philip replied, more knowledgeable about the speed of gossip than she might suppose, especially after his few weeks' sojourn in London. The news of the rich nabob's presence in town had sped among the *ton* as though it had been borne upon the very air.

However, Philip's main concern was not so much that the villagers might gossip about him, as that they might reveal his identity to Madeline before he found an opportunity to tell her himself. The possibility of something like that happening had been brought home to him that very morning when he visited the Frome cottage. Willem had been acquainted with old Horace Balenger for about sixty years, and the moment he looked upon Philip's face, the weaver had perceived the family resemblance.

"So," the man had said by way of greeting, "you be the nabob, I'm thinking."

Philip had not yet dismounted, and when the gelding felt his master's sudden surprise, he bobbed his massive head ominously, prancing about in a nervous manner. "Whoa, boy. Steady."

Actually Philip managed to control the steed's disquiet much more easily than he governed his own. "How did you know?" he asked, not bothering to deny his identity.

"It be something in the eyes, sir," the old man said. "Any as knew t'grandfather, they 'ud see the likeness same as me."

Although Willem had promised to keep his tongue between his teeth about the nabob's presence in the village, Philip was loath to rely for very long upon the man's ability to keep such a choice bit of gossip to himself.

Philip knew he had to tell Madeline who he was, and he knew he had to do it soon. But when? He had been pondering that very question earlier, when Quint and the ladies joined him on the bridge. Today was not the proper time, however, and the riverbank was not the proper place. Not with Quint and Miss Priscilla only a few feet away.

Privacy was needed to explain the circumstances that had prompted him to deceive her. And because Madeline would be angry—and justifiably so—they needed to be in a place isolated enough so she could not take flight before Philip had time to explain the whole story. A carriage ride would serve the purpose admirably. The only unanswered question was how to get her to ride out with him.

"Speaking of the nabob's arrival," she said, bringing his thoughts back to her last statement, "how long before that 'connoisseur' of beautiful women makes his appearance?"

"Sooner than you might expect," he replied.

"I? I assure you, I have no expectations whatsoever regarding the man."

"Perhaps not," he said, "but one never knows what fate may have in store."

At her questioning glance, Philip said, "I know the Balenger, and depend upon it, he will wish to make your acquaintance. If for no other reason than to congratulate you upon your efforts on behalf of the basket weavers."

At his words, her guileless blue eyes grew wide with surprise. "But I assure you, I wish no such singling out; not by the nabob or by anyone else. It is the cottagers who deserve Mr. Balenger's attention, and not I."

"Willem Frome would have me believe differently, for he sings your praises. According to that worthy, Miss Wycliff is solely responsible for the marked growth in their industry and, as a result, the increased food upon their tables."

Her pretty cheeks pink with embarrassment, Madeline stuffed the last of the goblets into the basket and began gathering her gloves and her reticule, obviously ready to end the picnic.

"I wish you will do something for me, please, Philip."

"Anything."

"If the conversation should ever arise with the nabob, please inform him that the cottagers' success with their baskets is due solely to their own talent and hard work."

"It shall be as you ask," he said, not wishing to distress her further.

Then, assuming a nonchalant air, he sighed and added, "Especially since I am certain the Balenger would much rather hear what *you* have to say of your neighbors, than what they have to say of you."

At his teasing tone, she relaxed, the pink in her cheeks fading, and her eyebrows lifted in question. "Oh, *would* he? And what have I ever said of my neighbors that would interest the nabob; or, for that matter, occasion such a smug look upon your face?"

Philip took a moment to make a minute adjustment to his neck cloth, as though the state of that item were of paramount importance. "I fancy the Balenger would be particularly interested to know that from your very own lips came the pronouncement that Lord Besford is a toady, and that Lady Besford cannot tell the difference between a prince and a frog."

Madeline choked back a laugh. "Philip! You know that remark was made in strictest confidence. You cannot mean to betray me."

"Certainly I do. 'Tis far too good a story to keep to myself."

"For shame. Have you no honor?"

He shook his head. "None whatsoever. You seem to forget that I am a buccaneer."

"But surely there is a pirate's code, or some such thing."

"I believe you are thinking of honor among thieves. Allow me to inform you, madam, even that is a myth. 'Tis but a clever-sounding phrase the brigands thought up to throw dust in the eyes of you law-abiding types."

Seeing she had finished smoothing her gloves over her fingers, Philip stood and extended his hands to assist her. "As for us buccaneers," he continued, "it may interest you to learn that our silence can be bought. We can be bribed."

"I might have known it would come to this," she said saucily. "With you being a pirate, and me being an unbelievably wealthy heiress, bribery was certain to enter the picture sooner or later." She laid her hands in his and allowed him to draw her to her feet. "What payment, I pray you, would ensure your silence? A million pounds? Two million? Name your price and have done with it."

Philip still held her hands in his, and as she lifted her face, a smile teasing her lovely lips, he was tempted to slip his arm around her slim waist and draw her close, to take his bribe right then and there.

She must have seen his thoughts in his eyes, for she lowered her gaze, then stepped back and eased her hands free of his grasp.

"Keep your two million," he said, bending to retrieve Miss Priscilla's reticule and shawl, where they had been left upon the blanket, "for I cannot be bribed with money. In any case, I had a different sort of payment in mind."

Before he could explain that his bribe would be for Madeline to agree to go for a drive with him, she was "Holloed" by her sister, who bid them hurry along to the bridge to witness the rainbow she and Quint had discovered.

"It is in the spray that hangs in the air, Maddy, just above where the water spills over those rough boulders. Come look."

"Coming," she answered.

Biting back his words of frustration, Philip offered Madeline his arm, and within seconds they had joined the others on the bridge.

After the rainbow had been suitably admired, Philip passed the shawl and reticule to Priscilla. Then he expressed his gratitude to that young lady for helping him entertain Quint. "For I fear his stay at the Hall has been deadly dull."

The visitor would not allow it to be so. "I have had much to occupy my interest. At the Hall . . . and elsewhere." If the smile he directed at Priscilla was not particularly subtle, neither of the Wycliff sisters found anything to dislike in the gentleman's words or his manners.

"Oh, there is much to beguile the hours here in Little Easton," Priscilla informed him. "For instance, my sister and I would not dream of missing the monthly assemblies. Would we, Maddy?"

"Certainly not," she answered promptly. In truth, Madeline had ignored the last three or four assemblies without experiencing any noticeable feelings of deprivation, but the entreaty in her younger sister's eyes was not to be ignored. "One must always find the assemblies amusing."

"By Jove," Quint said, "do you, perchance, know the date of the next gathering, Miss Wycliff?"

Priscilla answered for her sister. "I believe it is tomorrow evening."

"Famous! If I can procure a subscription, may I beg a dance, Miss Priscilla? And one of you, too, of course, ma'am."

In an act of charitable hospitality, Miss Priscilla said she would do her best to keep one or two places on her card available. "But only for country-dances," she warned him, "for I am not yet allowed to waltz in public."

"Of course not. I quite understand, and I shall be honored to partner you in whatever dance you will grant me."

While the younger couple were engrossed in giving and receiving such information as would insure Mr. Devon's arrival at the assembly, the foursome crossed over the bridge, with Philip slowing his pace so that he and Madeline fell back a ways from the others. His goal, to have a word with her in private.

Once again his plans were thwarted by Miss Priscilla. He was on the verge of proffering his invitation for the drive, when the damsel chose that exact moment to ask her sister if they still had time to stop in at the draper's shop.

"I believe so," she replied.

By that time, they had reached the spot where the geese had heralded their arrival earlier, and Philip dared go no farther. Afraid someone in the town might recognize him, he took his leave of them, saluting first Priscilla's hand and then Madeline's, taking the latter all the way to his lips.

"Until we meet again," he said. Then he tipped his hat, made them a bow, and strolled back toward the bridge.

Chapter 9

True to his word, Mr. Devon escorted the ladies to the draper's. And once inside the two-story brick building, the young gentleman was no less faithful in completing his pledge to give his opinion on the proper blue for the ribbons.

Availing herself of one of the seats ranged along the counter, Madeline stared at the rear wall with its ceiling-high shelves, upon which were stacked bolt after bolt of material—from the lowliest calico to the most delicate of silks. While she sat thus, looking without seeing, lost in thought, Priscilla and Mr. Devon sauntered among the aisles, commenting upon the laces, fans, and other such *fol lols* as struck their fancies.

When they finally chanced upon the ribbons and the precise color was found—Quint remarking that it was a perfect match for her lake blue eyes—Priscilla motioned to Mr. Truckle, the cloth dealer, that she had made her selection.

His scissors suspended from a chain around his neck, the draper removed a string from his pocket, and gauging by the various knotted sections of the string, measured the exact amount of ribbon Priscilla requested. Then, as soon as the cost of the purchase was entered in his book, the merchant coiled the ribbon around a card to keep it from wrinkling, presented it to Priscilla, then bid his shop lad bring the ladies' gig around to the front of the building.

Within minutes the Wycliff sisters had exchanged their good-byes with Mr. Devon, and were back on the road to Wybourne; Madeline once again tried to coax Comet to any speed exceeding a walk, and the gelding blithely ignored all her entreaties. Priscilla, normally quite happy to beguile the trip with chatter, was unusually silent, a circumstance that suited her older sister's own wish for a few moments to reflect upon their afternoon.

Neither lady interrupted the other's thoughts until the gig approached the gray stone entrance to Balenger Hall. As before, they both turned to look past the open iron gate, but again, there was nothing to see but the carriageway.

"What think you of him?" Priscilla asked.

Madeline felt the heat rush to her face. She had hoped to escape this catechism until after she had had time to reflect upon all that had happened today. Perhaps, she told herself for the millionth time, she should not have allowed her younger sister to be in Philip's company—after all, she knew her mother would disapprove. Yet Madeline knew him to be a fine man, and though not a gentleman, he was well mannered, thoughtful of her comfort, and sensitive to others' feelings; he was even concerned that Bertha Ramsbury might have suffered some ill effect from young Master Balenger's revenge with the frog.

For her part, Madeline had never met a man—gentleman or not—who so completely met her criteria for what a man should be. However, she did not wish to discuss these feelings with her sister.

Turning the tables, she inquired, "What did *you* think of him?"

Priscilla sighed. "I think he is the handsomest man I have ever seen. Do not you?"

"Yes," she answered softly, "I do."

"And his smile. Maddy, have you ever known any other man whose smile was so pleasing? So absolutely guaranteed to set a female's heart to fluttering?"

Her answer was a bit breathless. "No. I have not."

"Nor have I. Everything about him is well-favored. From his wide shoulders and his healthy physique to his beautiful eyes."

Madeline nodded her head, in total accord with her younger sister's observations, and not at all surprised that Priscilla had been as awed by Philip's rugged, piratical good looks as she had. And why should she not? Any woman must find Philip devastatingly handsome.

"His eyes are so revealing of the man inside, do not you agree, Maddy?"

"Oh, yes. Absolutely. And when he looks at you, you feel as though there is no one else around but you and him."

"You noticed it, too," Priscilla said, sighing. "And such a rich, warm brown."

"Gray," Madeline said.

"No. They are brown. I took special pains to be certain I was correct. And when we were in the draper's, I spied a ribbon that exact shade of brown. I even teased him about buying it. Quint said he got his brown eyes from his father's side of the family."

"Who did you say?"

"Quint." Mistaking her sister's surprised tone for one of censure, Priscilla said, "Oh, Maddy, please do not tell me I must go back to calling him Mr. Devon, for I declare it would be prodigiously difficult after an entire afternoon of calling him by his name."

Madeline almost laughed aloud. *What a fool I am.* Her

sister was not enumerating Philip's masculine charms, but Mr. Devon's. And why should she not? Quint was an unexceptional *parti,* and one perfectly suited to Priscilla's age and circumstances.

Not at all like Philip and Madeline.

"You may continue to call him by his name, Priscilla— just guard your tongue at home. You do not want to give Bella ammunition to use against you."

"No, I do not. Thank you for the warning. How wise of you to have thought of it. Though, why anyone, especially Bella, should disapprove of Quint is something I do not understand. He has much more to recommend him than our brother-in-law."

"A truth we cannot expect Bella to appreciate."

"Perhaps," Priscilla offered shyly, "we should not mention the nuncheon. Unless Mama asks, of course. I should not wish to tell her a falsehood. Even though," she added, sitting up very straight, with her chin lifted defiantly, "I have nothing to be ashamed of. After all, Quint is a respectable gentleman, and I was chaperoned by my very own sister."

And your sister's not-so-respectable friend. Calling herself a coward, Madeline said, "You may depend upon it, little sister, *I* shall say nothing of this afternoon."

If the two ladies remained quiet upon the subject, the same could not be said for Mr. Devon. Upon entering the taproom of the Green Knight some few minutes after seeing the ladies to their gig, that gentleman immediately bombarded Philip with his observations on the beauty, wit, and charm of Miss Priscilla Wycliff.

"Is she not exquisite, Philip?"

"To be sure. A diamond of the first water."

"And not the least bit set up in her own conceit."

"No. Not a bit of it. A very pretty behaved young

lady. Miss Wycliff had told me previously that her sister was a beauty, and I see she spoke the truth."

"Quite," agreed his young friend.

While Quint stared off into space, presumably lost in his reminiscences of the beautiful Priscilla, Philip made a methodical, though unobtrusive, survey of the dark-paneled room. He had asked his guest to meet him back at the Green Knight for a specific reason, so he could observe the men who patronized the only tavern the village boasted.

Having requested the innkeeper to bring him a fresh ale as a signal should any stranger enter the place, Philip raised the original mug of the strong home brew, sipping at the warm liquid to make it last. With the lid lifted and the tankard to his lips, he took the measure of each of the half dozen men who were seated upon the settles that flanked the massive fireplace. From the easy cama- raderie, and the laughing insults aimed at whichever of their number won at their game of shove halfpenny, Philip assumed all these men were known to one an- other, and from their rough smocks, he supposed they must be local farmworkers or basket weavers.

Whatever their occupations, not one of them had the look of a criminal. Nor did any of them put Philip in mind of the kind of villain who would threaten a house inhabited only by women.

Mr. Devon reclaimed Philip's attention, stating his de- sire to attend to the matter of the subscription to the as- sembly. Since the assemblies were held in the ballroom of the hotel, he had merely to sign his name in the book and pay his subscription for either the one occasion or the entire year. The young man had only just excused himself and gone in search of the proper person to pay when the landlord, a short, and exceedingly portly fellow with a jovial countenance, delivered a fresh tankard of ale to the table.

He set the pewter mug in front of Philip. "The ale you ordered, sir." Leaning down as if to wipe some spillage from the surface of the stained oak, he added, "A bloke as was here last evening be taking a seat over in the far corner. A nasty-looking type, if you was to ask me. But you said any stranger, sir, and he be that. Don't know as I heard him speak a civil word to anyone. Kept to himself, he did."

Philip slid a sovereign across the table. "For your trouble."

Under pretext of wiping the table again, the landlord pushed the coin back toward Philip. "My brother be one as got hired up at the Hall yesterday. And grateful he be, sir, as are we all. If there be ought I can do for you, you have only to ask. Name's Webber. Joachim Webber, at your service, sir."

Nodding in response to the landlord's offer, Philip watched as Webber waddled back over to his place behind the bar. Lifting the lid of the fresh tankard and raising it to his lips, Philip looked over the mug at the newcomer to the room. The stranger was as the landlord had described him, definitely a nasty-looking type. An ex-pugilist from the look of him, with his overly developed upper body and his broken nose and misshapen left ear.

Unlike the local men in their smocks, the stranger wore a coat—a short garment of coarse weave and indeterminate color—that did not quite meet across his barrel chest. A faded neckerchief was tied loosely around his thick neck, and a woolen cap was pulled low on his forehead. Sitting with his back to the wall, as if cautious about who he let behind him, he drank his ale without looking to right or left, avoiding eye contact with the other patrons.

When Philip set the still-full tankard down upon the table, he was surprised to have it whisked away and another set in its place. Webber was back. "There be another one," he said, wiping his hands down the sides of his blue apron, "just as big as t'other, but not so mean-looking. And this one's got a silver tongue in him. Chatting up one of the maids, he is, and asking questions. Heard him ask the way to the Hall."

Keeping his voice low, Philip asked, "Where is he now?"

"Still out there palavering to the lass, like as not."

Philip got up and strolled across the room to the bar, then continued to the door that opened into the inn's reception area. Pausing in the doorway, he spied a blond-haired man of about thirty engaging in what appeared to be flirtatious chitchat with a fresh-faced, willing young maid who was given to rather high-pitched giggles.

"Lah," said the girl, batting her dusky lashes at the stranger, "how you do run on. I b'aint all that pretty."

"Would I lie to you?" replied the man. "You country girls wear the blush of the rose upon your cheeks. Put the very flowers to shame, and that's a fact. I tell you truthfully, no city girl can hold a candle to you."

The newcomer was built not unlike the surly stranger in the taproom, only this man wore a neat, though inexpensive, brown driving coat and carried a tan beaver hat and driving gloves. But most interesting of all, a red vest showed beneath his coat.

Philip had been in London long enough to recognize a Bow Street Runner when he saw one. The detectives had been given the name "red breasts" due to their vests, but even without that identifying garment, Philip would have known who he was. There was about all the runners a certain brawny toughness, but they were also canny fellows, with an instinct for their jobs. Not only were they competent at tracking those who wished not to be found, but they were also adept at asking the right questions to aid in their search.

With seemingly very little effort on his part, the detective had induced the girl to furnish him with information regarding the likeliest place to encounter gypsies. Then he added, "And might there be any cottages untenanted, lass, or any empty shepherd's huts in the vicinity. For the way I see it, a fellow can't be too careful these days. Me, I've learned it's a good thing to know the places to avoid. 'Timmy,' me sainted mother was used to say, 'keep away from bad company.' And that's what I try to do.

" 'Course," he added, reaching up and giving the edge of the maid's mobcap a playful tug, "me mother never said I was to stay away from the pretty girls."

"Get away with you now," she replied with a giggle.

"Cruel as well as beautiful," he said, putting his rather large hand over his heart, as if wounded. "But I interrupted you, my beauty, you were saying something about empty huts . . ."

Stepping back over to the bar, Philip inquired of the tapster if he could hire one of the private parlors for an hour.

"Yes, sir," Webber replied. "Be you awanting summit to eat, sir?"

"No, another time perhaps. For now, I wish you to do me another service."

"Anything, sir."

"The man talking to the maid, please ask him to wait for me in the private parlor. When he is there, come back and tell me, for I do not wish anyone to see me talking to him."

Fortunately for Madeline's composure, neither she nor Priscilla were required to prevaricate regarding the picnic or the length of their stay in the village. As it happened, their sojourn was of less interest to their mother and sister than it might normally have been, principally due to the preoccupation of those two married ladies with their own interests.

Mrs. Wycliff had spent the better part of the day sequestered in her room, lounging upon a couch with pillows behind her back, a copy of Maria Edgeworth's *Vivian* in her hand, and a plate of currant buns on the small table just inches from her elbow. As for Arabella, that young matron spent her day stretched out upon her bed, dividing her time between bouts of crying, bemoaning the fact that her husband was not with her, and jumping at every noise for fear the person who had made the threat upon her life might have gained entrance to the house.

As a result, the conversation at that evening's dinner table consisted solely of Priscilla's plans for the assembly the following evening, omitting, of course, any mention of the young gentleman to whom she had promised a country-dance or two.

"I think I shall wear my blue," she offered for the entertainment of her listeners. "And perhaps I shall arrange my hair in a classical style, using my new ribbon. What say you, Maddy?"

"I am persuaded you will look lovely."

Priscilla giggled. "Silly. I was not begging for compliments. I mean, what will you wear?"

"Oh." Not having any reason to suspect this assembly would differ from the others she had attended for the past eight years, Madeline could not work up much enthusiasm regarding her wardrobe. "My pink sarcenet, I suppose. It is the most comfortable when one is obliged to sit for hours at a time."

"But surely you mean to dance?"

"Not without a partner, I do not. The last time I attended the assembly, I sat out all but one reel, and for that I had the dubious pleasure of being partnered by Squire Sandingham—an experience, I promise you, not unlike being pulled left and right by a well-meaning plow horse.

"And I pray you," she added, before Priscilla could retort, "do not think to tempt me with the curate, for you must know, that worthy cannot get through half a set without treading upon one's toes. I have not yet recovered from the Boulanger we danced last September."

"Maddy, you goose, I—"

"Nor, I warn you, will I allow you to suggest I stand up with old Mr. Braithwaite. I tell you to your head, should that septuagenarian approach me, I shall call for the landau immediately and leave you to get home however you may."

Giggling at her sister's teasing, Priscilla was shocked into silence when Arabella jumped to her feet, her movement so agitated she caused her chair to fall to the floor behind her.

Bella looked from one sister to the other, her quivering lips informing them that she was near to the breaking point. "I cannot credit my ears. Have you both lost your minds? How can you think of dancing, when the morrow might well find us all lying murdered in our beds?"

As it transpired, the inhabitants of Wybourne were spared any homicides during the night, but the next morning Madeline was awakened earlier than she would have wished by a scratching at her bedroom door.

"Come in," she mumbled groggily.

Not waiting for a second invitation, Tess hurried into the room, quickly closing the door and leaning her back against it as if to bar any who might have followed her there. "Oh, Miss Maddy!" she said, her voice trembling,

"Mrs. Jinks sent me up. Her not knowing what else to do, and me neither. Not with Jem gone to the blacksmith's, and for all we know, mayhap lying dead on the road with his throat—"

"What are you talking about? What has happened?"

"A man," she answered. "Near the stable. Maeve saw him when she went to pick some chives from the kitchen garden. 'Big as a house,' she said he was."

Madeline sat up quickly. For just a moment, a frisson of fear held her in its grip, then she recalled that the gypsy boy had said they had three days. He had come just two days ago, so the day of reckoning should be tomorrow.

Of course, the person who sent the boy could have grown impatient and decided upon today, but the most logical conclusion was that he was trying to frighten them further, make them more biddable the next day—collection day.

Realizing that this was just the kind of low trick guaranteed to succeed with a household of females, Madeline threw back the covers, angrier now than she had been frightened before. "Is Maeve all right? Did he threaten her?"

"No, miss. He stepped behind a tree when he spied her, and Maeve come running back to the kitchen. But fair scared out of her wits, she was. And me and Mrs. Jinks not much better off, what with all this talk of cutting throats."

The last two words were almost inaudible as the maid lifted her apron to her face and began to cry. "Ohhh," she wailed, "why did Miss Bella have to go and marry Lord Townsend?"

So that little secret was out. Madeline might have guessed the servants would know everything that was said in the house, for only fools believed it possible to keep private family matters from reaching the kitchen.

Sighing, she padded barefoot across the room and put her arm around the sobbing maid's shoulders, then led her over to sit on the little stool at the dressing table. After waiting a minute or two for the girl to compose herself, she asked, "What did Jinksie want me to do about the man? Shoot him? Even if I had a pistol, which I do not, I would not know how to use it."

"Oh, no," Tess said, wiping her tears, obviously finished with her bout of nerves, "Mrs. Jinks knows you can't do nothing about that man."

"Then I do not understand why—"

"It's on account of me not ever going into the wood," she explained. "Maeve goes there all the time, but she's having the vapors, so she's of no use to anybody. And since Mrs. Jinks is too old to go traipsing about, she said for me to run over to the Hall and ask somebody to go for the squire—there's men aplenty over there mending and fixing up and such. Only I don't know my way through the woods. Mrs. Jinks thought as how you could tell me how to go on."

After a few moments of reflection—moments in which Madeline remembered Philip's promise that she had only to send him word if she saw anyone hanging about the place—she hurried over to the clothespress and began pulling out stockings, drawers, and a shift. Quickly stepping into each article, she then slipped her night rail over her head and tossed it toward the bed.

"Bring me my brown dress, Tess, and help me fasten up the tapes. Then get my walking boots."

"What do you mean to do, Miss Maddy?"

"I shall guide you to the Hall. I cannot allow you to go alone."

"God bless you!" the girl said, hurrying to do as she

was told. Two minutes later, paying little heed to the fact that her hair still hung down her back in its nighttime braid, Madeline hurriedly tossed her blue cloak around her shoulders, fastening the frog as she ran down the back stairs to the kitchen.

Cautiously opening the kitchen door, she peeped out into the early-morning stillness, but all she saw was a smattering of fog that lingered near the edge of the wood. When she was satisfied the man was not close enough to grab either of them, she warned, "Stay close behind me, Tess, for I mean to run as fast as I can."

Matching the deed to the word, Madeline lifted her skirts almost to her knees and sped down the footpath past the kitchen garden, then over the bluebell-covered stretch of land beyond the garden and into the wood. Tess stayed close on her heels. By the time they accomplished the mile and a quarter to the brook, Madeline's breath was coming in gasps and her side felt as though someone were sticking a giant pin in it. At the stepping-stones, she made certain no one had followed them; then she crossed over to the Balenger side of the boundary.

Because the maid's breathing was even more ragged than her own, Madeline kept her pace to a brisk walk as they passed her sheltered bower and the spot where she had found Philip and Mr. Devon fly fishing the last time she had come this way. Not being fortunate enough to encounter the men a second time, she followed a slight indentation in the grass that she hoped had been made by them, and therefore the proper direction to the Hall.

Her instincts served her well, and within fifteen minutes Madeline saw the brick stable ahead. Even in her breathless state, she could not help but notice the improvements to the structure. Someone—or perhaps several someones—had expended many hours of work upon the building, for it possessed a new roof, reglazed windows, and double doors newly rehung and freshly painted.

Hurrying inside the stable, Madeline found a lad of about fifteen mucking out one of the stables. "Good morning," she said, frightening the young boy into dropping his pitchfork.

"Lawks, miss! You fair give me a fright, you did."

"I beg your pardon," she said, quickly scanning the half dozen empty stalls until she spied Mr. Devon's pretty sorrel mare. Two stalls farther down, she found what she had been looking for, the large, beautifully proportioned Arab she and Philip had ridden. "That gelding," she said, "do you perchance know where to find his owner?"

"T'black? Aye, miss," he answered, his eyes big as coat buttons. "T'horse be the property of—"

"Please find the owner for me," she instructed, "and tell him I need to speak with him right away. The matter is most urgent."

"Aye, miss."

Pulling his forelock respectfully, the lad bent to retrieve the pitchfork; after standing it in a corner of the stall, he hurried out of the stable and up the gravel path.

Madeline followed him only as far as the mounting block. Then, as soon as she saw the lad disappear around the bend in the path, she sat down to catch her breath and wait. She could relax now, knowing that Philip would be there shortly.

It never occurred to her to wonder *if* Philip would come to her, only when he would arrive.

While sitting upon the mounting block, Madeline could not help but remember the last time she had done so. It was the day Philip took her up before him on his beautiful black horse and held her against his chest, his muscular arm around her waist. How wonderfully free she had felt as they all but flew toward Wybourne, and how exciting it had been to be held so close to him. She had never experienced such feelings before, and—

Her musings were halted by the sound of footsteps crunching upon the gravel path, and when Madeline looked up, she saw Philip running toward her. Her heart began to pound at the sight of him.

He must have come straight from his bed, for his white linen shirt was only partially tucked into his buckskin breeches, and the neck of the shirt stood open, revealing his strong bronzed throat and a good portion of his chest. His crisp, sun-streaked hair was uncombed, and his handsome face bore the dark shadow of yesterday's whiskers.

"What has happened?" he asked even before he reached her.

Overcome by shyness at seeing him *en deshabille* so shortly after recalling the excitement of being in his arms, Madeline was forced to swallow before she could speak. "One of the maids saw a man in the garden," she said finally. "You told me I should come to you if anything of that nature occurred."

"You did the right thing."

He stood only inches away from her, looking unbelievably tall and indescribably masculine, and when he stepped closer and took both her hands in his, it was almost as if some of his strength was transmitted to her. His hands were strong and warm, and for just a moment, Madeline had to fight a nearly overwhelming urge to fling herself into his arms, to feel their warmth and strength enfold her.

"What can you tell me of this man?"

She shook her head. "I can tell you nothing. It was one of the maids who saw him."

Reluctantly slipping her hands from Philip's firm, re-

assuring grasp, she glanced toward the stable, where
Tess sat upon the grass, her knees drawn up to her chest
and her head resting upon her folded arms. "Tess,"
Madeline called, "will you come here please?"

Coming immediately, Tess dropped a curtsy to Philip.
"Good morning, sir."

Philip nodded, then asked, "Can you tell me anything
at all about the man you saw?"

" 'Twas Maeve who saw him, sir, but she said he was
big."

"Anything else? Did she mentioned his clothing, perhaps?"

"Yes, sir. She said he was neatly dressed. Wore a curly
beaver, he did."

"And a vest?" Philip offered helpfully.

"Yes, sir, I believe she did say summit about a vest.
Red, I think it was."

Smiling at the girl, Philip thanked her for the information. "If you will, I should like to speak to your mistress
for a moment."

"Yes, sir." Dropping him another curtsy, Tess returned
to her place by the stable.

Turning back to Madeline, he said, "I know the identity of the man your maid saw, and you have no reason
to fear him. He is a Bow Street Runner."

Still somewhat bemused by the respectful way Tess
had responded to Philip, especially since servants were
usually very quick to detect the social class to which a
person belonged—be he gentry or laborer—Madeline
was slow to ask, "How could you know that?"

"Because I sent him."

"You sent him? But why?"

"I could not think how else to insure your safety until
your father's return. I knew you would be angry, for it

was an unconscionable intrusion into your affairs. However, I—"

"Angry?" *He had been worried for her safety.* Madeline swallowed to ease the tightness that obstructed her throat. No one had ever voiced such a concern for her before, not even her parents. It was an idea that left her feeling surprisingly vulnerable.

"Philip, I . . ." She felt the tears well up in her eyes and threaten to spill over, and not wishing to make a spectacle of herself, she turned her face away. "Thank you," she said quietly.

Philip had seen the sparkle of moisture in her beautiful eyes and known a moment of discomfort. He had been prepared for her anger, but not for her tears. He had not meant to hurt her. But at her softly spoken words, he knew all was well. She had accepted the appearance of the detective, not as an intrusion, but as the gesture of friendship he had meant it to be.

"Thank *you*," he said, more relieved than she would ever know, "for not being offended."

When she turned back to him, it was with a watery smile that put Philip in mind of a ray of sun shining through the rain. And as if that was not enough to send him staggering, when she lifted her face, the hood of her cloak fell away from her head, calling his attention to the loose braid that hung down her back and the myriad of wispy curls that framed her lovely face. Seeing her thus, he realized that like him, she had come straight from her bed.

At the thought of Madeline lying beneath the covers, her skin still warm from sleep, her hair in its braid, and her soft body clothed only in a flowing night rail, his pulse quickened and began to throb in his veins. He had to stop himself from reaching out and catching the long braid, for he felt a burning need to loosen those plaited tresses and feel their silken texture ripple through his fingers.

"How could I be offended by anything you chose to do?" she said. "Did I not come to you for help?"

Still lost in his fantasy of discovering the texture of her hair, still absorbed in the heady contemplation of unfastening a part of her that she had bound, it was moments before Philip realized she had spoken. As to what she had said, he had not the least idea. "I beg your pardon. I did not—"

"That is quite all right," she replied. Though her voice sounded calm, her pink-tinged cheeks betrayed her embarrassment as she gently tugged her braid from his hands and tossed the partially loosened hair behind her shoulder.

Looking from her rosy face to his outstretched hands, Philip realized that he had acted out his thoughts! *My God!* Fearful of what he might do next, what other liberties he might be tempted to take, he backed away from her.

With her eyes downcast, she pulled the hood back up over her hair. "I fear I did not take time to make myself presentable. I hope you will forgive the way I look." Having said this, she stood and stepped away from the mounting block.

With superhuman effort, Philip recovered his composure. "Come," he said, offering her his arm, "I will escort you back to Wybourne."

Chapter 10

Since the footpath required that they walk single file, Philip took the lead, followed by Madeline, then the maid, Tess. Most of the walk was accomplished in silence, with him cursing himself with each step he took for being an idiot and not controlling his desires. Although, if the truth be told, he had been holding a tight rein on those baser instincts almost from the moment he met Madeline that day he had pulled her out of the brook.

Quite frankly, if he had given in to only half his fantasies, she would have far more to blush about than a loosened braid.

However, before he could put anything of that nature to the test, he had to tell her who he was. And for that revelation, he needed privacy—a treasure as frustratingly elusive as pirate's gold. He was beginning to think his only hope might be to act the buccaneer he claimed to be and steal her away.

When they reached the brook and could abandon their single file, Philip decided now was the time to request that she drive with him. Before he could speak, though, Madeline asked him to please send the bill for the Bow Street Runner to her father."

"There will be no bill," he said.

"But Father will—"

"You would please me by letting the subject rest."

Madeline decided to do as he asked, but only because she could think of no logical argument to dissuade him. Logical? She had to stop herself from laughing, for she had not had a rational thought in her head since she had spied Philip running across the gravel, looking so male, so powerful, so capable of defeating any foe.

Furthermore, she was still reeling from the soul-shattering experience of having him slowly reach out and capture her braid, his strong fingers gently freeing the strands. The way his hands had felt in her hair. The suggested intimacy. The way he had looked at her; the darkening of his gray eyes making her breath catch in her throat. The combination of sensations had weakened her knees, so much so that she marveled she had been able to walk.

"Besides," he continued, giving her a teasing smile that under normal circumstances she would have been able to return, "there is another matter I would much prefer to discuss."

Madeline breathed deeply, hoping the act would calm her, not at all certain she possessed the fortitude to discuss a subject whose prelude was such a heart-stopping smile.

"Yesterday," he said, reclaiming her thoughts, "we were discussing the payment of a bribe. Unfortunately we were interrupted before I could tell you what I would consider a fair recompense for my silence."

"So," she said, relieved that he had returned to their earlier foolish banter, "you have decided upon your price?"

"I have. It remains only for us to agree upon the time of payment."

"Not so fast, if you please. *I* have not yet agreed upon the price. And I warn you, I shall not stand still for extortion. I admit to a certain trepidation, for when a buccaneer sees fit to whistle down the wind an offer of a million pounds, one must question what dreadful substitution he has in mind."

"I hope you will not find it so very dreadful," he said, his tone serious once again. "I merely wished to take you for a drive."

A drive. No! Philip could not have asked a price more impossible for her to pay. He must know it was out of the question for her to drive with him, to be seen alone with him in public. If he did not know it, she certainly did.

Madeline had been left in no doubt as to her mother's feelings upon the subject of her daughter associating with a man from a lower social class, and long acquainted with her father's animadversions upon those he termed *jumped-up commoners*, she could well imagine his reaction if Philip should appear at their door. And if her father were still from home, it would not be beyond Arabella to suggest—no, demand!—that Philip go around to the tradesmen's entrance.

"Is it so difficult to give me an answer?" he asked.

Yes! "No."

"Then will you drive out with me? I had something I wished to say to you."

"Whatever it is, Philip, can it not be said here?"

"No, it cannot. The matter is rather complicated and will require some time for a proper explanation." He glanced toward Tess, who had walked over to the brook's edge but was still close enough to hear anything spoken above a whisper. "Also, what I have to say is of a personal nature, and I feel certain I would plead my case more effectively if I could speak with you privately."

Personal nature? Plead his case in private?

Madeline's lungs seemed to come to a complete halt,

so breathless did she feel. Surely Philip was not about to ask . . . Surely he did not mean to make her an . . .

She strove to remain calm, a nearly impossible feat, especially when she recalled the intimate look that had smoldered in his eyes when he had held her braid in his hands. A look to which some primitive longing inside her had willingly responded.

My God! It is true. Philip means to make me an offer of marriage.

"What say you?" Philip asked.

"Say?" she stammered.

"Will you drive with me?"

Needing time to compose her turbulent thoughts, she hesitated.

"If you are worried," he said into the silence, "that I shall spill you into the hedgerows at the first turn, you need not. As strange as it may seem, there are horses and carriages in India, and I have driven many of them. Furthermore, I flatter myself that I am a credible whip, and I assure you that if you will trust yourself to my care, I shall return you to your home in one piece."

"I . . ."

"This afternoon?" he pressed.

Grabbing at the first excuse that popped into her head, Madeline said, "I cannot this afternoon. I shall be busy getting ready for the assembly."

If Philip thought it odd that a full afternoon was needed to prepare for a local assembly, he was polite enough to keep his thoughts to himself.

"Another day, perhaps?" she suggested.

"Of course," he said quietly, his manner reserved. His thoughts—whatever they were—he kept hidden from her by the simple act of lifting his gaze to observe a falcon coasting in the air above them, thereby denying Madeline the opportunity to search his expressive eyes.

Unaccustomed to anything save friendliness from him, Madeline was more distressed by Philip's reserve than she would have thought possible. She wanted desperately to say something to put the teasing smile back upon his lips, but she could think of nothing that would not also encourage him to believe she was desirous of hearing his proposal.

Unable to think what was best to do, she took the coward's way out and called to Tess to hurry along. "For Jinksie will be worried that we have come to harm."

"That she will, Miss Maddy. Be fair walking a trough in the floor by now, or I miss my guess."

"Shall I see you to your home?" Philip asked.

Madeline shook her head. "We will do nicely from here. Now that I know the runner is looking out for our safety at Wybourne, I feel positively brave."

Offering him her hand, she said, "I thank you, Philip, for"—her throat tightened, making it almost impossible to continue, and the breath she drew was noticeably ragged—"for everything."

The women's reception in the kitchen at Wybourne was quite gratifyingly dramatic, with Mrs. Jinks falling upon first Madeline's neck, then Tess's, and calling up prayers of thanksgiving for their safe return. But from the way Maeve hurried into the kitchen, her mobcap askew and something akin to panic in her face, the housekeeper's emotional welcome was a pallid affair in comparison to the high drama being enacted in the back parlor.

"Burnt feathers!" Maeve said, the high pitch of her voice suggesting that the thin cord holding her hysteria in check was near breaking. "Miss Priscilla be awanting burnt feathers. The sal volatile b'aint working."

Startled by this news, Madeline said, "What is wrong with my sister? Is she ill?"

"She be lying upon the settee in a swoon, Miss Maddy."

"Priscilla?"

"No, miss. It's Miss Bella—or Lady Townsend, I should say—what's on the settee. Miss Priscilla, she be running back and forth between Miss Bella and the mistress. The mistress be having palpitations and megrims and I don't know what all, on account of the man waiting outside to murder us all!"

Out of patience with such Cheltenham drama, Madeline bid Tess tell Jinksie and Maeve about the man's true identity while she saw to her family. "You may disregard the request for burnt feathers," she added. "I think a tea tray would be more in order, for I doubt anyone has thought of food since this entire fiasco began."

Delaying only long enough to divest herself of her cloak and drape it over the back of a chair, Madeline hastened to the parlor to confront the chaos that reigned in that small chamber. And chaos it was.

Bella, still attired in her night rail and a flowing wrapper of willow green lawn festooned with ell upon ell of blond lace, lay stretched out upon the yellow brocaded settee, her arm across her eyes. Quite near the settee, a glass lay discarded upon the threadbare carpet, its spilled contents making an ever widening stain. The unsuccessful sal volatile, Madeline presumed. She might have thought her sister asleep, had it not been for the soft moans issuing from the lovely matron's lips every two or three seconds.

As for Mrs. Wycliff, that lady had forsaken moans in favor of shrill cries interspersed with animadversions upon the character of both her own husband and the husband of her daughter—the former for being from home when he was most needed, and the latter for being the principal wreaker of the havoc that would at any minute culminate in their demise.

Priscilla, on her knees beside her mother's chair, held that lady's dimpled hand, patting it and offering up such logical comments as were guaranteed to annoy Mrs. Wycliff and prompt her to further strident predictions of doom.

Upon perceiving Madeline standing in the doorway, Priscilla gasped, then abandoning her mother, she dashed across the room to throw herself into her eldest sister's arms. "You are returned!" Having voiced the obvious, the young lady gave herself the pleasure of bursting into tears. "I was afraid he . . . he had somehow contrived to capture you."

"Shh," Madeline said, patting her lachrymose welcomer upon the shoulder, "I am fine, silly goose."

After allowing Priscilla a few moments of watery release, Madeline disengaged herself from her young sister's stranglehold. "Have done, there's a good girl, for I have something to tell you. All of you."

Priscilla did as she was bid, with only a telltale sniff to testify to her outburst. At the same time, Mrs. Wycliff gave up her screams, and Arabella sat up, all three ladies waiting expectantly for the latest word of the outside world.

"We have nothing to fear from the man in the garden," Madeline said. "He is a Bow Street Runner hired to insure our safety."

Priscilla, the first to react, uttered a most unladylike word. Then, disgust writ plainly upon her face, she declared stoutly, "Of all the tempests in a teapot! I do not know how I came to be born into such a family."

Mrs. Wycliff's trembling hand went to her heart. "A runner, you say? And he is here to protect us?"

"Of course!" declared Bella, jumping up from the sofa, her face radiant, her voice bubbling with exhilaration. "Oh, my wonderful, wonderful husband!"

Having rhapsodized thus, Bella executed a pirouette in the middle of the room, the willow green wrapper billowing out behind her like a boat in full sail; then she fairly floated across the carpet to embrace her mother, saluting that lady upon either tearstained cheek. "This is all Townsend's doing, Mama. He must have seen to the hiring of the runner before he left town. Oh, I should have known he would not forsake me. But I shall scold him soundly for giving us such a fright, the dear, wonderful man!"

Staggered by this total misreading of the situation, Madeline drew breath to disabuse her middle sister of the notion that Lord Townsend had spared so much as a moment's thought for the safety of either his wife or her family. However, upon further consideration, she decided against carrying out that piece of revenge. What purpose would it serve? Bella would be hurt, and Madeline would be obliged to explain just who *had* hired the runner.

Honesty compelled her to admit that the latter circumstance weighed more heavily with her than the former. But whatever the reason, Madeline held her peace.

Claiming the headache—a condition that would be true soon enough if she did not immediately absent herself from her mother and Arabella, and the quite revolting sight of those two ladies congratulating one another upon the fortunate addition of Lord Townsend to the family—Madeline quit the crowded parlor and escaped to her bedchamber. She needed privacy in which to contemplate what had happened between her and Philip. She needed quiet to consider all he had said, as well as what she had been afraid to let him say.

Now, without his disturbing presence to befuddle her brain, Madeline wondered if she had perhaps overreacted to Philip's words. *Personal* need not, of course, refer to something pertaining to her. He could have meant he wanted to discuss a matter that applied to him, and him alone.

But he had said he thought he could plead his case better in private. *Plead his case.* How many kinds of cases did a man plead?

Aside from the obvious instance of a barrister in a court of law, the only example Madeline could think of—other than that of making an offer of marriage—involved begging someone's pardon for an offense committed. In that particular situation, the offender would certainly wish to explain his misdeed—or, plead his case—preparatory to making amends.

But, of course, that circumstance did not apply here, since Philip had done nothing for which he needed to beg her pardon. It was just the reverse, for she had called upon him for help almost from the moment they met, petitioning for favors as though she had every right to do so. And every time, he had stood her friend—honest and trustworthy.

That left only a proposal of marriage.

Stretching out upon the bed she had left much too early that morning, Madeline allowed herself a moment to reflect upon the honor Philip paid her in wanting her for his wife. And it was an honor. Not only was it a tribute she had never received before in her five and twenty years, but it was also one she had not expected to know. Just being asked by a man like him warmed her heart. In fact, the mere thought of being married to Philip, of being the recipient of his passionate kisses, his intimate embraces, did more than warm her heart. It positively set that organ afire!

No! No! She must put such seductive fantasies from her mind. They would not do. No matter the pleasure she would derive from knowing Philip's embrace, or the joys she would realize from sharing his life, such a marriage—such a *mesalliance*—was out of the question.

After grabbing one of the linen-covered bed pillows and plumping it with such fervor she came within Ayme's ace of dislodging the downy feathers from the ticking, Madeline turned onto her side, groaned aloud, then hugged the maligned pillow to her chest as if it would shield her defenseless heart from the undeniable truths that attacked it.

If the circumstances had been different, she could have begged heaven for no greater gift than to be loved by Philip.

But, alas, the situation was one as would put her beyond the pardon of her family. Priscilla would never disown her, of course. Madeline knew that as surely as she knew how *she* would react if their cases were reversed. As for Bella and her parents, however, they would not be so forgiving. Just thinking of their cold snubs turned Madeline's skin to gooseflesh.

Also, there was the matter of her actions ruining Priscilla's chances for an advantageous marriage.

But what of *her*? What of her own chances for happiness—a full life? Did Madeline not deserve an opportunity to realize her dreams?

And what of her heart?

That, of course, was the one question whose answer she knew without equivocation. She loved Philip. It was that simple. It was that profound.

How it had happened—even *when* it had happened—she did not know. Somehow, while she was merely enjoying their pleasant encounters, Philip had managed to insinuate himself into her heart—slowly, gently, until the mere sound of his voice had begun to arouse within her an unbidden, aching desire. Being with him had exposed a need, a longing she had never admitted before, not even to herself. And it was a need that only Philip could satisfy.

In her mind and in her body, Madeline knew that he was the person meant for her alone. From the instant they met, she had felt some indefinable connection between them. A rapport. An understanding. A bond, almost as if they were counterparts of the same soul.

"Too, too foolish," she muttered, turning onto her back and pulling the pillow over her face as if to smother all such fanciful thoughts.

Even supposing there was any validity to this feeling of a connection to Philip, Madeline could never accept his hand. The world cared little for such capricious notions as corresponding souls. If she married him, she would be obliged to forsake her family, her friends, her very way of life.

But the alternative was to forsake her heart.

"Can I do that?" she whispered. "Can I put Philip from my thoughts? From my dreams? From my memory?" The softly spoken questions seemed to wind their way into the deepest, most vulnerable part of her, causing a heaviness to form inside her chest and tears to well up in her eyes.

Unfortunately she found no answer to her query. Neither tears nor logic prevailed, though both waged an endless battle inside her brain.

At the end of the afternoon, when Priscilla knocked at her door to inform her it was time to dress for the assembly, Madeline had come to no decision as to what she should answer if and when Philip was allowed to plead his case.

If only he were a gentleman. But he was not, and there

was no point in repining over what could not be changed. One thing was certain: Madeline must either depress Philip's interest for all time and never see him again, or else she must follow her heart and encourage him to pay her court.

She knew what her heart wanted her to do.

Chapter 11

For his part, Philip spent a productive afternoon seated behind the massive, leather-topped desk in his book room, going over his new bailiff's recommendations for the renovations needing to be done to the cottages of the Balenger tenant farmers. Also, a tract had arrived offering advice regarding a system of crop rotation. As well, Philip read every word of a multipage list of suggestions upon such fascinating subjects as the addition of lime, chalk, or marl to improve the quality of the animal manure used for the crops.

With such earthy matters demanding his attention, and completely unaware that he had thrown Madeline into a soul-shattering abyss of indecision, Philip had put aside for the time being his annoyance at the fact that the lady had turned down his request to go for a drive. Much inclined to believe he would never find the proper time and place to apprise her of his true identity, he had decided to put it to the test at their next meeting, and have done. The longer he waited, the more difficult the task became, and he had no desire to wait another day.

"A thousand pardons for the interruption, sahib."

Philip calmly looked up from the papers he held, accustomed to the silent approach of the mahogany-skinned giant in his soft, leather slippers.

"What is it, Singh?"

"A visitor," the servant replied, bowing his turbaned head and extending toward his master a silver salver upon which reposed a card bearing the insignia and the London address of Sir John Fielding's Bow Street Runners.

"Excellent," Philip said, setting the papers on the desk, "the other runner has arrived. Show him in, please."

A minute later, the inscrutable Singh ushered in a man whose appearance varied little from that of the detective who was even now keeping himself well hidden in the shrubbery at Wybourne. Both runners were large, capable-looking men, both neatly dressed and sporting the red vest. The major difference was in their hair color; the second man had dark hair where the first detective's hair was blond.

"Sir," said the runner, unable to stop himself from gaping at the retreating servant in his knee-length white coat and his gathered, burgundy silk trousers.

Philip allowed the detective his moment of awe—it was always thus with newcomers. Then he said, "I expected you yesterday."

"Begging your pardon for the delay, Mr. Balenger, but I was finishing up another assignment—one not unlike the circumstances you mentioned in your letter."

Motioning him to a red leather wing chair, Philip said, "How so?"

The runner disposed himself in the chair before answering. "You'll understand, sir, that I can't mention any names, on account of our clients wanting to maintain their privacy. So . . ."

"Yes, yes. Tell me what you can."

"Well, sir, there is a certain gaming hell in town where the sharps—*Greek banditti* some folks call them—gather to fleece the young cubs who come to town thinking they know it all. 'Course, sometimes the flats ain't so young.

Sometimes they're established gentlemen who've become persona non grata at the gentlemen's clubs, if you get my meaning."

"I understand the sort to whom you refer."

"The usual procedure at the hells," the runner continued, "is for the sharp to let the flat win some trifling amount during his first visit or two; then, once the fish swallows the bait and is convinced he can win his fortune at the tables, the real playing begins. The owner of the hell understands the baiting period, but once the flat starts losing, the house expects to receive a certain percentage of the take. Trouble is, sometimes the sharps get to thinking the owner is one of the flats, and they try to diddle him as well. A real mistake, as one *banditti* discovered a fortnight ago."

The runner lowered his voice. "The fool was found floating in the Thames with his throat cut from ear to ear."

Philip left his place behind the desk and strode about the book room. He had been concerned before that Madeline not be frightened; now, however, with the knowledge that a murder had been committed, his concern turned to foreboding. He stopped his pacing and perched on the edge of the desk, near the runner. "And you believe the murder of that cardsharper may have some bearing upon this case?"

"Like I was saying earlier, the assignment I just finished was not unlike this situation here. It involved a young cub who had given his vowels to a gaming hell sharp—a sharp recently discovered in the Thames. Last week the cub's family contacted Bow Street. Seems the lad's mother was accosted when leaving Hatchard's lending library on Piccadilly. The lady was threatened with violence if the vowels were not paid within three days."

"Damnation!"

"Just so, sir."

"And the outcome to this sordid affair?"

"The young man's father paid the debt. Afterward, the entire family made a hasty removal to their country seat. My job was to retrieve the vowels for the gentleman."

Philip slapped his hand against the top of the desk. "And that was all? There were no arrests for this extortion?"

The runner shook his head. "Weren't no proof of any extortion, sir. Nothing but a young man's debts of honor held by a third party, a Mr. Flynn, who claims to have bought them all legal and aboveboard."

"The gaming hell owner," Philip said through clenched teeth.

"You catch on fast, sir. Had an alibi for the night of the murder, did Mr. Flynn. Seems half of London saw him sitting in his box at Haymarket."

"Naturally. But what of the person who threatened the cub's mother?"

"Because the lady was too frightened to give us a good description of the man, we were unable to apprehend that villain."

Philip walked across the room and pulled the bell for a servant. Almost before his fingers left the pull, the door was opened.

"Yes, sahib."

"Singh, see that my dress suit is laid out."

Bowing, the giant said, "It shall be done, sahib."

Returning to the desk, Philip gave his orders to the runner. "I wish you to guard a certain lady. No matter where she goes, you are to keep her within sight at all times. The other runner is even now standing guard at the lady's residence. He can watch the house and its occupants, but I want you to make protecting Miss Madeline Wycliff your personal mission. Do I make myself perfectly clear?"

"Perfectly clear, sir. And where will I find Miss Wycliff?"

Philip removed from his pocket the gold watch that had once belonged to his father, then flipping open the intricately scrolled case, he looked at the face. "Sometime within the next two hours, the lady and her younger sister are to attend this evening's assembly at the hotel. From the moment she leaves her home, I want you at hand."

"We have less than two hours before the dancing begins, Maddy," Miss Priscilla Wycliff warned her sister, who lay stretched out on her bed, a pillow held over her face. "Come along, do, for I have brought you a tray with some sandwiches and a cup of tea. You have not eaten all day, and this will be your last opportunity. I am certain I do not need to remind you what the refreshments are like at the assembly.

"Ugh!" the voice beneath the pillow answered.

Correctly interpreting this remark to be a judgment upon the dry cakes and insipid negus thought adequate to be served at an assembly, Priscilla lifted the pale gray teapot with its golden yellow rose pattern and poured the hot liquid into the matching, translucent cup. "Here you are," she said, handing the cup to her sister, who had tossed the pillow aside and slid to the edge of the bed to swing her limbs over the side. "Drink up, for Bella's abigail has kindly consented to dress your hair this evening."

"Bella's maid? But why would she offer to do such a thing? From the moment they arrived, that female has spared no pains to let everyone know that she is accustomed to serving in much more exalted establishments than Wybourne."

"Yes," Priscilla agreed, "we all know she was used to be the dresser for the fashionable Viscountess Wrothby. Tonight, however, she has offered to assist you, having decided to look upon you as a heroine."

"What nonsense is this?"

"The abigail, a female of perspicacity, believes it is *you* whom we must thank for the reassuring presence of the Bow Street Runner. She has worked for Lord Townsend since his marriage to Bella, and no more than you or I does the woman believe his lordship responsible for the hiring of our guardian angel."

Madeline felt her face grow warm at her sister's searching look, but in no mood to exchange confidences that would only remind her of Philip and the decision she must make, she took refuge behind the teacup, bringing the thin porcelain to her lips and sipping slowly.

"But," continued Miss Priscilla when her sister vouchsafed no further information regarding the miraculous appearance of their burly protector, "I do not mean to tease you. Unlike the people of Troy, I shall not put my nose where it does not belong, although it is as obvious as a wooden horse that someone other than our esteemed brother-in-law hired the runner, and equally obvious that you know who that person is and why he did it. However, I shall allow you your little secret, confident in the knowledge that you always do the right thing."

Wishing she felt even a modicum of that confidence, Madeline blushed again. "Priscilla, I—"

"Drink," she interrupted. "I said I would not tease you, and I meant it."

Hearing a scratch at the door, Priscilla hurried to open it. "Here is Tess with your hot water. Make haste and finish your sandwiches, there's a good girl, so you will have plenty of time to freshen up before Bella's starched-up maid comes to perform her magic upon you."

"By all means," Madeline replied, biting into a wafer-thin sandwich. "I shall certainly wish to be turned out as magnificently as possible when I take my place along the wall with the chaperons."

If Priscilla noticed the sarcasm in her sister's voice, she made no comment, merely squealing when she spotted the position of the hour hand on the small brass clock above the mantel. "Yikes! I must run. I have to see to my own toilette, for I mean to try a little magic of my own this evening."

As the door closed behind her young sister, Madeline lifted another of the sandwiches, took several bites, then did as she had been instructed and made use of the hot water, freshening up in preparation for the arrival of the fashionable viscountess's former dresser.

Madeline had not long to wait, for the very superior servant arrived within a few minutes. After bidding her heroine be seated on the stool before the oak dressing table, the woman arranged the looking glass so she could see in it. Then she began her work upon her subject's coiffure.

As for the promised acts of magic, Madeline would rather have called them strokes of genius. With nothing more than a pull here, a lift there, that toplofty personage transformed Miss Wycliff's hair into a work of art—a sophisticated, yet deceptively simple, masterpiece.

After first unbraiding the long, thick plait and brushing the light brown tresses until the red-gold highlights shone in their depths, the woman then drew the hair back from Madeline's face, not bothering to part it, only catching it high in the back and securing it with two large combs. Then, after twisting one strand around the

whole and securing it, the maid flipped the remainder
over her hand, then flipped again—much as a baker
would twist a roll of dough—and in a matter of seconds
voila! a neat, thick, shiny figure eight of hair was being
secured to the back of Madeline's head.

Without either asking or waiting for approval, the
woman used the brush to release a curling tendril just in
front of each ear.

"Now, miss," she said, taking a quick look through
Madeline's nearly empty jewelry box and producing a
pair of pearl earbobs that had once belonged to Mr.
Wycliff's grandmother, "I think these should do very
nicely."

While Madeline obediently fastened the jewelry to her
lobes, then stared in a somewhat bemused state at the sophisticated stranger in the glass, the maid went to the
door and opened it to Tess, who held Madeline's freshly
pressed pink sarcenet across her arms.

"Oh, Miss Maddy," Tess began, her eyes wide as
saucers at the effect of the elegant hairstyle upon the
slender face and graceful neck, "you look a picture, you
do. Like a princess."

"That will do," remarked Bella's superior maid, taking
the dress and dismissing the country lass as though she had
every right to do so. Then, holding the gown so Madeline
could step into it, she said, "If you please, miss."

Only after Madeline had allowed the dresser to assist
her into the deep pink silk that had already seen a year's
worth of assemblies and parties, did she notice the refur-
bishing done to the gown. For starters, the gauze over-
skirt had been removed, and in its place a scattering of
pale pink rosebuds had been embroidered upon the unpretentious skirt, with similar embroidery where the delicate material was gathered beneath the wearer's bosom.

And there was much more bosom visible! A rather

startling amount, Madeline decided as she slipped her arms into the puffed sleeves.

The neckline that had previously reached to the hollow of her throat, now scarcely covered her breasts. As she waited for the tiny buttons in the back to be fastened, she stared at the rounded swells of creamy flesh now exposed. She would have protested the immodest show of skin had the maid not immediately tied a pink velvet riband around her throat. Embroidered upon the riband was a single, beautiful rosebud, and Madeline was so impressed with the effect of the simple adornment that she could only gaze quietly into her looking glass.

The slender young lady who looked back at her, dressed in her simple yet becoming gown and her elegant coiffure, surprised Madeline into silence. She could not believe the creature was herself.

"You look quite lovely, miss," said the maid.

"Thank you," Madeline said almost inaudibly. Then, with more enthusiasm, "and thank you very much for all your work."

"A pleasure, miss. And if I may be so bold, I wish you a lovely evening."

"Thank you. I shall do all within my power to—"

"Maddy," Priscilla said, opening the bedroom door after the briefest of knocks, "what think you? Should I carry the Norwich shawl I usually wear with this gown, or would the new cashmere with the silver floss fringe be more becom—" The vision in palest blue gauze, with the matching celestial blue ribbon threaded charmingly through her blond curls, stopped just inside the room. "Oh, Maddy," she whispered, awe in her voice. "You look beautiful."

The two Wycliff sisters stood just inside the marble-tiled vestibule at Wybourne, waiting for the arrival of the landau that would transport them to the Green Knight Family Hotel for the assembly. Both ladies were in good spirits due to their confidence in their appearance, and if only one of them was ecstatic at the promise of an evening filled with dancing and admiring beaux, the less excited sister did not let the prospect of sitting out most of the dances dampen her own spirits.

As Madeline listened for the sound of the horses' hooves, she was surprised to hear instead the unmistakable swish of satin. Turning at the sound, she was even more startled to discover her middle sister descending the staircase.

Beautifully coiffed, and wearing a topaz necklace and matching earrings, Bella was dressed in a gold satin gown worthy of a London ball. From the magnificent cut of the dress, which set off her figure to perfection, to the cascade of titian ringlets that brushed her alabaster shoulders, Lady Townsend was the epitome of the London society matron.

Priscilla was the first to recover from the shock of seeing her sister. "What is this, Bella? For days you have done nothing but mope around the house, and suddenly here you are looking like a duchess on her way to opening night at the opera. Surely you do not mean to accompany us to so rustic an entertainment as the Little Easton assembly?"

Bella laughed as though amused by Priscilla's question. "Silly child. Of course I mean to go with you. As you say, I have suffered from a fit of the dismals since my arrival, but now I feel quite myself again. Now that I have had word from Townsend, I—"

"You heard from your husband?" Priscilla asked. "I did not know that Jem had brought us any mail. Did *La Belle Ensemble* arrive as well?"

"There was no mail," Bella explained, as though

speaking to one lacking in wit. "When I said I had had word from my husband, I referred to the arrival of the runner Lord Townsend hired for our protection."

"Ah, yes," Priscilla remarked dryly, "so thoughtful of your husband, to be sure."

Arabella found nothing amiss in the comment, absorbed momentarily in twitching a fold of her satin skirt into place. "I only hope this dress may not be ruined before we reach the village." Then, looking from one sister to the other, she said, "If I am to arrive uncrushed, I shall need the entire seat. Both of you will have to sit with your backs to the horses."

Madeline was about to give her sister a scathing setdown, but before she could get the words out, Priscilla performed the task. "An excellent suggestion," said that young lady, "for we would not wish to crowd you. In fact, Bella, lest you think us selfish, please allow me to offer you the entire coach. Maddy and I will content ourselves with running in the dust behind."

Ignoring the absurdities of both her sisters, Madeline opened the entrance door and stepped outside just as Jem drew the landau up. "Good evening," she greeted the coachman. Well aware that Jem could not leave the horses, she opened the coach door for herself and climbed into the ancient vehicle, taking her place on the forward-facing seat.

"Come," she called to Priscilla, "sit next to me, for Lady Townsend wishes to have an entire seat to herself."

"In just a moment," replied the irrepressible Priscilla. "I have one more thing to say to Bella."

The red-haired beauty glared at her younger sister, her hazel eyes afire with anger. "I believe you have said quite enough, miss! You are an impertinent chit, thoroughly lacking in manners, and you need discipl—"

"I give you fair warning," Priscilla said, her words

softly spoken, for Bella's ears only, "do not ruin this evening for Maddy or for me. Not unless you are desirous of knowing what a cup of negus would do to the front of that lovely gold satin."

The ballroom at the Green Knight was lighted by two chandeliers at either end of the long chamber, and in addition to the dozen or so candles that blazed overhead, numerous sconces provided additional light along the walls. At the top of the room was a flower-festooned dais just large enough to accommodate the pianoforte and two chairs—one each for the two violinists—while at the bottom of the room, lined against the wall, chairs had been arranged for the comfort of the chaperons and any young ladies unfortunate enough not to have a partner for the dance in progress.

The three Wycliff sisters, having entered the ballroom just as the musicians sounded the chords for the opening cotillion, were too late to participate in the first dance. However, they contented themselves with surveying the couples in the various sets to ascertain which of the ladies present might be wearing a new gown or hairstyle.

Of course, with the public event being open to any who could pay the subscription price, not all those performing the figures of the cotillion were of the gentry. Numbered among the dancers in the sets, Madeline recognized the sons, daughters, nieces, and nephews of many of the town's merchants. As well, she spied Squire Sandingham's daughter, Lizzy; Reverend Hazlip's daughter, Sarah—now Mrs. Colquit; and several other members of the local gentry. Also, to her surprise, Madeline spotted Lord and Lady Besford alamanding their ways through the set.

"Is that Bertha Ramsbury?" Bella asked. "I declare I have not laid eyes on her since before my wedding."

If an amused look passed between Madeline and Priscilla at the sight of Bertha Ramsbury's raven curls, their sister chose to ignore it, unaware of the episode of the tiara and the long-ago birthday party when Philip had set the frog in the spoiled girl's hair.

The moment the cotillion ended, Bella made her way straight to Lady Besford's side. Meanwhile, Madeline and Priscilla strolled toward the chairs at the bottom of the room, speaking to several of their acquaintances as they walked. They had only just found places on either side of Mrs. Colquit, who was fanning herself after the exertions of the dance, when Priscilla spied Mr. Devon entering the room.

The young lady's sudden stillness caught Mrs. Colquit's attention. "I say," she remarked behind her fan, "who is that extremely handsome young man?" Noting the sudden blush that rose to Miss Priscilla's cheeks, the lady quit her teasing and addressed her next question to Madeline. "Friend of the family, I presume."

Speaking behind her fan as well, Madeline said, "The acquaintance is quite recent, Sarah. The gentleman is visiting at Balenger Hall. He is Mr. Quintin Devon, of Stavely."

"Stavely? A lovely old property, Stavely. In all the guidebooks, don't you know. Your Mr. Devon must be Lord Holmes's heir."

Although Madeline found this whispered exchange of particular interest, her sister heard not one word, for Priscilla's attention was entirely caught by the young man. And though she blushed prettily, she did not see fit to lower her gaze, watching instead as Mr. Devon searched the sea of young ladies in their blues, yellows, pinks, and lilacs. When his fruitless scrutiny of the dancers led him to investigate the chairs along the wall, the sudden smile upon his face told the interested damsel that he had been looking for her alone.

As he made his way to her, Priscilla did not feign disinterest in his arrival. Instead she returned his smile with one brilliant enough to inform any who wished to know that she was as pleased to see the gentleman as he was to discover her.

"Good evening, Miss Wycliff. Miss Priscilla," Quint said, bowing to each in turn. "May I compliment you both upon your looks this evening?"

Madeline shook the gentleman's gloved hand, then waited until he had finished shaking her sister's hand before presenting him to Reverend Hazlip's daughter. "Sarah, may I present Mr. Quintin Devon? Sir, allow me to make you known to our friend, Mrs. Colquit."

"Your servant, ma'am."

Exhibiting the pleasant, unaffected manners Madeline had remarked before, the gentleman inquired if he might be allowed to write his name down upon each lady's dance card.

"I see the third set is a waltz, Miss Wycliff. If I promise not to tred upon your toes, may I have the pleasure of partnering you for that dance?"

Permission granted, Mr. Devon wrote his name beside two dances on Madeline's card, one on Mrs. Colquit's card, then two upon Priscilla's—one of them the set just beginning, which was a quadrille. Excusing himself to the other ladies, he and his willing partner hurried to take their places among one of the squares where a fourth couple was wanted.

"A very handsome pair," Mrs. Colquit remarked, raising her eyebrows knowingly. "Priscilla would make a lovely baroness. Do not you agree, my dear?"

Madeline concurred completely with that sentiment. In fact, she was of the opinion that her sister would make a *beautiful* baroness, although modesty forbade her from voicing such a viewpoint. Contenting herself with a smile, she changed the subject by asking her friend a polite question about Mr. Colquit.

"My husband," replied the lady pleasantly, "has never been much of a hand at dancing, and he roundly refuses to attend any function where there is not a card room to keep him occupied." Putting her tongue in her cheek, she continued, "Bertha and Lord Besford were so kind as to take me up with them in their coach. Such condescension, don't you know."

As if conjured up by the mention of his name, that supercilious gentleman suddenly appeared before them, bowing and begging a dance from Mrs. Colquit, who had the grace to blush a fiery red. Madeline was hard-pressed not to laugh aloud at her friend's near faux pas.

Looking at Lord Besford's thin, unhandsome face and noting the amount of buckram padding needed to give his foppish coat even a semblance of manly shoulders, Madeline was reminded of the picnic and her very rude observation regarding Bertha Ramsbury's husband and his resemblance to a toad. Hiding her smile behind her fan, Madeline bid the couple enjoy their dance.

Once she was alone, she entertained herself by watching the dancers and tapping her slippered foot to the spirited tune. Lost in the music, she did not see the tall, well-built newcomer enter the room, though she was instantly aware of his presence.

Unlike Mr. Devon, Philip did not scan the dancers but looked immediately to the bottom of the ballroom where Madeline sat. At first sight of him, her blood began to pulse in time to the music. Then their eyes met, and in that instant everyone else seemed to vanish.

They were alone. Just Madeline and Philip and the

music. Her heart fluttered inside her breast. Breathlessly she watched as he came toward her, slowly, beguilingly.

She had never seen him look handsomer. He wore a beautifully tailored coat of dark blue superfine that fit his broad shoulders to perfection and gave his gray eyes the look of cobalt, while his cravat and waistcoat, both pristine white, emphasized the sun streaks in his thick hair.

At some point Madeline became aware of the dozen or so chaperons who occupied the other chairs. It was difficult not to notice them, for the ladies seemed positively abuzz with excitement. One after another, they whispered behind their fans, their gazes fastened upon Philip.

Unable to hear what was being whispered, yet instantly frightened that the ladies meant to rebuff Philip—or even worse, denounce him as a laborer and have him thrown from the premises—Madeline rose from her chair and walked toward him, her hands outstretched. Even when she heard someone gasp at her boldness, she was undeterred. Let the old tabbies label her as fast. She could not—would not—let them abuse Philip.

He took her hands, and at his strong, warm touch, they were alone once again.

His eyes searched hers as though they would plumb the very depths of her soul. Then he spoke softly, his voice warm, caressing. "You look exquisite."

"So do you," she answered, bemused.

He chuckled, and a dazzling smile crinkled the tanned skin around his eyes, making Madeline's heart pause in mid beat. In that moment, all her earlier indecision fell away. Looking into Philip's smiling face, feeling his strong hands holding hers, she knew the world was well lost for this man.

She loved him. And if he loved her in return, nothing else mattered.

She would drive out with him tomorrow—never mind her family's disapproval—and when he asked her to marry him, she would accept his proposal.

Her decision made, Madeline felt as though blinders had been lifted from her eyes. How could she have doubted, even for a moment, the rightness of becoming Philip's wife? Nothing could insure her happiness as completely as spending her life with him. All her doubts gone, she felt almost giddy, as though she had partaken of too much wine, and happier than she had ever been in her entire life.

"Will you dance with me, little mermaid?"

"Oh, yes," she answered breathlessly. The musicians had struck up a waltz, and Madeline was much inclined to think she would have swum the Indian Ocean for the chance to feel Philip's arm around her waist.

Still holding her right hand in his left, he placed her left hand on his arm, then slipped his right hand around to her back. Before she had time to assimilate the delicious sensations resulting from being held thus, he waltzed her into the midst of the dancers.

He danced the way he did everything else, with grace and assurance. In perfect time with the music, they glided across the floor, Philip leading her with strength yet gentleness, and Madeline delighting in matching her step to his.

With her hand upon his arm, she felt the rhythmic rippling of his muscles, and something deep inside her responded. Her mind and body were awash with sensations she had not even known existed. If she had been giddy before, now she was completely intoxicated.

As they whirled around the room, neither of them spoke. For Madeline's part, she needed no words. It was enough to be here, in the arms of the man she loved. When she finally raised her face to look up at Philip, and heard the quick intake of his breath, she knew that what she felt in her heart must have been revealed in her eyes.

"Madeline," he said, a note of surprise in his voice, "I—" The music stopped, and whatever he had meant to say was, of necessity, cut short.

When the gentlemen began escorting their partners back to their chaperons, Madeline reluctantly stepped away from Philip. She would have returned to her chair if he had not placed his hand beneath her elbow and stayed her steps. "I must speak with you," he said, his tone resolute. "Now if you please. I have been interrupted too many times, and what I have to say cannot wait another moment. Is there some place we can be alone?"

Never having been posed such a question before, Madeline had no knowledge of those secluded little nooks where lovers held secret trysts, hidden from prying eyes. She was trying desperately to think of some alcove close by where they might secure a moment of privacy, when she noticed Bella standing near the entrance to the ballroom. Her sister was beckoning for Madeline to come to her, and from the agitated look upon Lady Townsend's face, the matter was urgent.

Madeline's mind already distracted, she begged Philip to excuse her for just a moment; then, without waiting for him to escort her across the room, she hurried to her sister. "What is amiss?"

"You might well ask," Bella replied, her voice hushed yet shrill. Her eyes were feverishly bright and her color was high with emotion. "Come into the cloakroom, for I do not wish anyone to overhear us."

Madeline gave one quick glance over her shoulder to where Philip stood. He was no longer alone, having been joined by Priscilla and Mr. Devon, but his gaze followed Madeline as though he wanted to come to her. Wanting that very same thing herself, she was in complete sympathy with his feelings. However, something had upset Bella, and since Madeline could not ignore the possibility of its being important, she followed her sister to the cloakroom.

The moment the door closed behind them, Bella turned on her. Her voice was no longer hushed, and her face was livid with anger. "Such selfishness! I declare I would not have believed it, Maddy. Not even of you. Have you no consideration for your family? Never mind the havoc you will wreak upon me and my husband, you must know you are ruining all Priscilla's chances."

"You are speaking fustian, Bella. Whatever has befallen you and Lord Townsend is of your own making. I take no responsibility for anything—"

"Do not attempt to throw dust in my eyes, for I saw you dancing with him."

Him? Her sister must be referring to Philip, as Madeline had danced with no other. Ready to defend her beloved buccaneer against all enemies, Madeline said, "I warn you, Bella, I will not tolerate animadversions upon Philip's character. Nor will I be swayed by your opinion, for he is truly one of the finest men I have ever—"

"Philip!" Bella shrieked. "You call him by his name? I cannot credit my ears. You are too coming by half, Madeline. Have you no pride? Of course you have not, else you would not be so lost to all propriety as to steal your own sister's intended."

Ready to defend herself against the earlier accusation of being without pride, Madeline was thrown off balance by the quite ludicrous idea that she would—or could—steal her younger sister's intended. Where on earth had Bella gotten such a ridiculous bee in her bonnet?

Suddenly remembering the tavern belowstairs, Madeline asked, "Have you been drinking?"

"I? Do not be absurd!"

"I own, I would not have thought it of you, Bella, but what—other than imbibing in strong drink—could lead you to indulge in these histrionics and the quite foolish notion that I would harm Priscilla. Our sister has a partiality for Mr. Devon, true enough, but I doubt it has reached the point of a serious *tendre*. But even should that be the case, I have always treated the young man with the utmost—"

"You try to fob me off, but it will not do. I do not refer to that boy as our sister's intended, and well you know it. I am speaking of the nabob. Of Mr. Philip Balenger."

Madeline felt as if the ground had suddenly lost its solidity. Like a wave, the floor seemed to swell, then ebb, threatening to give way beneath her. "Who?" she asked, placing her hand on the wall to keep from falling. "Who did you say?"

"The nabob! Kindly refrain from playing off your missish airs with me. You know his name as well as I."

Madeline shook her head. "I . . . I do not know the nabob."

"Do you take me for a fool?" she shrieked, tossing her head in an angry manner that set her titian ringlets bouncing. "The entire company saw you practically run to him the minute he walked into the room. And the way you were making sheep's eyes at him! I tell you, Maddy, I was never so embarrassed in my life. All the old cats were whispering about the spectacle you were making of yourself. If it had not been my own sister, I would have found the exhibition quite as diverting as did everyone else."

"But he—the man I was dancing with—he is not the nabob."

"Of course he is, addle wit. He was spoken to in the corridor by a ferocious-looking man in a red vest, and I heard the man call him Mr. Balenger. And if that is not enough, Lady Besford recognized him. She asked him how he was enjoying his new horse. It seems he and Lord Besford bid against one another at Tattersall's last month. The nabob won out, naturally, his pockets being so deep. I believe Lady Besford said the animal was a black Arabian."

Philip had watched Madeline as she followed Lady Townsend to the cloakroom, and when the door closed behind them, he had experienced a moment of panic. The woman could ruin everything! When he had only just arrived at the assembly, and Lady whoever-she-was had introduced him to Lady Townsend, he had known he was in trouble. Recognizing the name as belonging to Madeline's sister, he knew he had to reach his mermaid and find a way to have a private word with her before her sister, or someone else, told her who he was.

Then he had entered the ballroom, and Madeline had come to him, looking so beautiful she had knocked his senses head over tail, and all rational thought had left his brain. All he could think of was taking her in his arms. Since waltzing was the next best thing to holding her, he had danced her onto the floor, forgetting everything but the blood that pounded in his veins as she yielded to him, following his lead. And when she had looked up at him, her eyes rivaling the brilliance of the stars, it was all he could do not to crush her to him and cover her enticing mouth with his own.

By the time he remembered his mission, the dance was ended and Lady Townsend was beckoning Madeline to her. Drat the woman!

He should not have come to the blasted assembly. He

had known that from the beginning. Nor would he have come, if he were not afraid for Madeline's safety. The moment the runner told him about the murder, Philip knew he could not let her spend the evening in such a public place, not without sufficient protection.

The runner was here, of course, but the man worked for hire. A stranger, the red breast might not be willing to give his life to protect a client. Philip, on the other hand, knew how bereft the world would be without Madeline. She was kindness itself. So protective of her young sister, as well as caring for the people of the village. And so gentle. Not to mention, funny and daring. She possessed so many admirable qualities that he could not count them all.

After Madeline left with her sister, Philip had been joined by Quint and Miss Priscilla, but the young lady had been claimed almost immediately by a new dancing partner. Reminded that he was promised to a Mrs. Somebody, Quint, too, hurried away. Once they joined the dancers, Philip went to stand in the corridor, just to the right of the ballroom entrance, to wait for Madeline's return.

Scarcely five minutes later, he saw the cloakroom door open again and both ladies emerge. While Lady Townsend hurried to the ballroom, her face set purposefully, Madeline approached the staircase leading to the ground floor. Even from where he waited, Philip could see that her face was ashen, and he thought he detected a slight quivering of her chin.

"Madeline," he said, stepping forward, his hand stretched out to receive hers. "My dear, you are overset, and I believe I know the cause. Please, may we have that private word now? If . . ."

He stopped, for she had not given him her hand, nor had she looked at him.

"We have nothing to say to one another that would require privacy, Mr. Balenger."

Mr. Balenger? Damn! The witch *had* told her!

"Little mermaid," he said softly, "won't you look at me? Please."

She did as he requested, although from the anguish he saw in her eyes, he almost wished she had not. He had expected anger. Even embarrassment. But not this hurt look, almost as if she had been betrayed. He had to stop himself from pulling her into his arms to comfort her.

As if she had read his mind, she stepped back. "The day we met," she said, her voice not quite steady, "you warned me that the nabob was a knave and a bounder. At that time, I believed you to be jesting."

She made a sound that might have passed for a laugh, but the serious expression on her face denied all humor. Then, after taking a deep breath, she squared her shoulders and lifted her chin. "Now, of course, I see that the jest was on me."

"No! Never. I promise you, Madeline, I—"

"Please," she said, the first spark of anger showing in her eyes, "make me no promises. I would not believe them in any case, for even a country simpleton like me cannot be fooled forever. Though, in all honesty, I suppose it was *I* who fooled myself. Such a gull you must have thought me."

"I thought nothing of the sort!"

Convinced he could explain it all if he could get her alone, he reached out to take her by the elbow, his destination the cloakroom she had just quit. But his fingers had no more than touched her arm, when he heard Miss Priscilla's voice. That young lady hurried from the ballroom, Quint just behind her, Lady Townsend following.

"Maddy, what has happened? Bella said you wished to go home."

"Yes. I . . . I have the headache."

Quint looked from Madeline's wan face to Philip's, *I told you so* writ plainly upon his countenance. "Is there anything I can do?" he asked.

Philip was not certain to whom he addressed that question, but Madeline shook her head.

"I wish only to go home," she said.

Philip noticed a brightness in her lovely eyes and knew that tears would soon be spilling down her satiny cheeks. The knowledge hit him in the chest with the force of a bludgeoning club.

As she stepped upon the top stair, he followed, not caring now who heard what he said. "Madeline. Please. I can explain. I vow, I never meant to deceive you, it was just—"

"I am a self-deceiver," she said, almost as if talking to herself. "And I have been such a fool."

Pausing for just a moment, she turned to speak to Miss Priscilla. "I am sincerely sorry for spoiling your evening, Priscilla. Please accept my apology."

Stepping past Philip and slipping her arm around Madeline's shoulders, the young lady bid her think no more about it. "I assure you, no apologies are necessary. We shall have you home in a trice."

As if something had just occurred to her, Madeline said, "I suppose I owe Lady Besford an apology as well. For I maligned her, you know. It is *I* who cannot tell the difference between a prince and a frog."

Chapter 12

"Ugh!" Mrs. Wycliff complained, setting the china cup in the saucer and pushing the offending vessel several inches from her breakfast plate. "This tea is stone cold."

"Let me get you another," Priscilla offered, rising from her chair and walking over to the sideboard on which reposed platters of basted eggs, braised kidneys, toast, and marmalade. Touching the silver teapot and finding it still quite hot, she poured the mahogany-colored liquid into a fresh cup, dropped in two sugar cubes, then carried the cup to her mother.

After several reviving sips, Mrs. Wycliff resumed her diatribe upon the trials suffered by herself as a result of the inconsideration of her offspring—principally her eldest and youngest. "What more, I ask you, must I be obliged to endure. First I am frightened quite out of my wits by villains, then—"

"But, Mama," protested Miss Priscilla, "surely you do not mean to lay that accusation at Maddy's and my door, for neither of us has a husband who gambles away his livelihood and that of his—"

"Mother!" Arabella squealed.

"Silence!" ordered their mother. Since none of her three daughters doubted to whom that instruction was issued, Miss Priscilla resumed her seat while casting a fulminating glance at her married sister.

"No husband, indeed," Mrs. Wycliff continued. "And no more shall you ever have one, my gel. Not if you continue in this quite unseemly manner. Picnics by the river! I declare, I shan't know where to look when next I pass any of our neighbors. Such disgraceful behavior. So completely wanting in conduct."

Receiving no response to this observation, the outraged matron turned to glower at her oldest daughter, who had spoken little since she entered the breakfast room. "And what have you to say for yourself, Madeline? Do not sit there as though the cat had absconded with your tongue. I would have an explanation from you, miss, for on your head rests the blame for this entire contretemps."

Madeline placed her fork beside the eggs and toast she had pushed around the plate but never tasted. No, she thought, the cat had not stolen her tongue. However, judging from the aching hole inside her chest, her heart was definitely missing. And the loss of that organ was her fault for being so foolish.

She wanted to scream in frustration at her idiocy, her self-deception.

True, Philip had deceived her regarding his name, but that was more an act of omission than commission. The notion that he wished to offer her his hand was her own invention. He had never said anything about matrimony. Try as she would to remember some innuendo, some double entendre meant to suggest he was desirous of a permanent relationship, she could think of none. Madeline could recall no word or gesture of his that indicated a desire to propose marriage.

He had asked her to ride with him. *A carriage ride.* Nothing more. Her fantasies had turned it into a *liaison d'amour.*

And that fantasy was a piece of folly she meant never to divulge. Not to anyone. Not so long as she lived.

Let her family continue in their belief that she was overreacting to being the object of an embarrassing jest. Better that they think her without humor than to know she had concocted the entire romance in her head, nurturing it without any assistance from the fiancé elect. Far better that they never suspect she had invented a lover, a love affair, and a proposal. Bad enough to know herself a fool, without apprising her family of the fact. If they knew, she would figure as the butt of family jokes for the remainder of her life.

No one need tell Madeline how often old maids figured as objects of derision in stories. When she was a child, she saw this happen to an elderly cousin of her father's, a lady who visited Wybourne twice each year. The cousin had no home of her own, so she divided her time between the houses of those relatives who agreed to her visits.

When required to spend a night at an inn, the fastidious lady insisted upon looking beneath the bed to assure herself that no refuse had been left there by the former occupant. The family, of course, repeated this story each time the cousin visited, insisting that she looked beneath the bed in hopes of finding a man hiding under there. "Any man would do," Mr. Wycliff used to say, his words lost amid the laughter of his audience, "for old maids cannot afford to be too choosy!"

Madeline still remembered the hearty laughs at the cousin's expense. She would never forget one time when the maiden lady overheard the remark and the laughter, nor could she forget the travesty of a smile upon the dear lady's lips as she tried to maintain her dignity.

"I am waiting," Mrs. Wycliff said, bringing Madeline's thoughts back to the present. "What have you to say for yourself?"

Taking strength from her memory of the elderly cousin's bravery, Madeline said, "I apologize, Mother, if my introducing Priscilla to a young man of wealth and breeding has put you to the blush. I had it directly from Sarah Colquit's lips that Lord Holmes's heir is a most eligible *parti*. Moreover, Sarah informs me that there have been Holmeses at Stavely for centuries."

Silence followed this artful revelation.

"Of course," Madeline continued, "I had no notion that you would consider the son of a baron beneath Priscilla's notice, otherwise, I would not have agreed to chaperon the two young people during the picnic. As for the neighbors, I cannot perceive why any of them should remark such an unexceptional outing. An alfresco nuncheon in broad daylight, in full view of any of the town's people who cared to notice . . . surely none but the strictest of sticklers could find anything to censure in that. Unless, of course, they were jealous of Priscilla's conquest."

Much struck by this view of the matter, Mrs. Wycliff considered her daughter's words while finishing off a wedge of toast slathered with orange marmalade. "A baron, you say?"

"So Sarah informs me."

"But what about the nabob?" Bella asked, looking challengingly at her mother. "We agreed that Priscilla should marry—I mean to say, meet—Mr. Balenger. Surely you have not forgotten our conversation, Mama?"

Before her mother could answer, Priscilla picked up the gauntlet. "Give over, Bella," she advised. "It is obvious you cherish hopes that I shall wed to oblige you. Allow me to disabuse you of that totally unfounded notion. Nothing could be farther from the truth. If and when I marry—be it to the baron's heir or the butcher's boy—the choice shall be mine alone, and any financial gain from the union will stay where it belongs, with *my* husband."

Naturally this declaration threw Bella into a fit of tears. As well, it visited upon their mother an attack of palpitations that would not be soothed until Tess entered the breakfast room with a plate of freshly baked currant buns, their sugar glaze still bubbly from the oven. The sweet, cinnamony aroma of the hot buns had a calming affect upon the matriarch, who declared herself in need of nourishment. "Bring the plate over here, Tess, for I am too weak to serve myself, and my daughters are too involved with their petty squabbles to spare a thought for my comfort."

After serving Mrs. Wycliff, the maid reached into the pocket of her white apron and removed a piece of folded paper bearing a blue wafer. Walking around to the other side of the table, she offered the missive to Madeline.

Madeline did not even look at the paper. Feeling the heat rush to her face, she lowered her gaze to her hands, which lay in her lap, the fingers laced together so tightly the tips grew cold.

"What is this?" Mrs. Wycliff asked, her words muffled by a large bite of currant bun. "What have you there?"

Bobbing a curtsy, Tess said, "Begging your pardon, ma'am, but it's a letter for Miss Maddy. One of the men from the Hall brought it a few minutes ago. Told me, he did, that I was to be sure Miss Maddy knew it came from Mr. Devon."

Not from Philip. Madeline let out the breath she had been holding. Then, releasing the death grip on her fingers, she took the note from Tess's unresisting hand. After breaking the sealing wafer, she scanned the dozen or so lines of masculine scrawl. When she looked up from the sheet, it was to find all three sets of eyes observing her.

"Do not keep us in suspense," Mrs. Wycliff instructed. "What does the young man have to say?"

"Mr. Devon has been so kind as to offer to drive me into the village today."

Communicating the remainder of the message to her youngest sister, she said, "It is Friday, and our friend remembered that the consignment of baskets goes to Bristol today. Thinking it might not be wise for me to drive to the village alone, he has offered me his protection."

"And do you mean to go?" Priscilla asked.

"I must. I have letters for the carter to deliver to the Bristol harbor master regarding our shipments. But I shall not call upon Mr. Devon for escort. I plan to take Jem with me."

When Mr. Devon arrived an hour later, Tess showed him into the front parlor where Priscilla sat, perusing a copy of Heideloff's *Gallery of Fashion*. Then the maid hurried to the steward's office to inform Madeline that the gentleman had arrived. Within a few minutes, Madeline entered the parlor, carrying her blue cloak over her arm.

"Miss Wycliff." Quint said, stepping away from where he leaned against the mantelpiece, then taking the hand she offered. "Once again you are to be commended upon your punctuality, ma'am. I only hope I have not kept you waiting."

"You have not, sir. But I must inform you that I mean to drive to the village with our coachman. Though I thank you for your thoughtfulness."

A blend of surprise and disappointment showed on the young gentleman's face, but after a moment's reflection, he bowed in acquiescence. "It shall be as you wish. I shall not press you. However, I will request one favor of you."

Madeline knew a moment's premonition. "One is foolish, sir, to grant favors before the nature of the request is known."

"Truly said, ma'am. Therefore, I shall honor your candor by not dissembling. I have come with a commission from one who is desirous of begging your forgiveness. May I beg your indulgence in allowing me to fulfill that commission?"

Unwilling to be rude to a gentleman who had shown her nothing but kindness, Madeline nodded her assent; then she watched as he reached inside his driving coat and withdrew a note sealed with a blue wafer. He held the folded paper toward her, but she made no attempt to take it from him.

"Two letters in one day. My, my," she said, hoping for a light tone, "I cannot remember the last time I received so much correspondence." Smoothing her kid driving gloves over her fingers, she said, "I think, however, that one letter is sufficient. You will oblige me, Mr. Devon, by returning the missive you hold to whomever may have penned it."

"The correspondent is Philip," he said quietly.

The mere mention of Philip's name was like a blow to Madeline's heart, but wishing to show Mr. Devon just how *not* heartbroken she was, she laughed softly. "How silly of Mr. Balenger, to be sure. You may inform him for me, sir, that while I was justifiably vexed with him for playing his little jest at my expense, I have now had a night to reflect upon the matter and find the entire episode much ado about nothing."

Mr. Devon's unsmiling eyes told Madeline he was not as convinced by her careless display as she might have hoped. "Is it your wish, Miss Wycliff, that I tell Philip you have forgiven him?"

Her throat felt painfully tight. "Yes." The word was spoken barely above a whisper.

When Mr. Devon offered the letter a second time, Madeline chose not to see it and turned to leave the room. Her escape was barred, however, by the entrance of Arabella.

"Maddy. I see you are still here."

"Not above another minute, however. I was just saying my good-byes."

"Do not go just yet. Mama and I have been discussing the matter, and we feel there is safety in numbers." Indicating the red cloak folded across her arm, she said, "I mean to accompany you to town. You and I will ride in the gig, while Mr. Devon and Priscilla follow us in his carriage."

Stepping past her startled sister, Bella offered the visitor her hand. "How do you do, Mr. Devon. So nice of you to lend us your protection."

The plan, a blatant attempt on their mother's part to throw the two young people together, pleased everyone but Madeline, who was suspicious of her middle sister's good-natured acquiescence.

"I will be but a minute," Priscilla promised happily, hurrying up the stairs as she spoke. True to her word, the young lady returned quite promptly, fetchingly attired in a sea green pelisse and a chip straw bonnet with matching sea green ribbons tied into a saucy bow beneath her right ear. If the ensemble bore none of the finesse of Bella's stylish crimson cloak with its white velvet lining, her escort seemed oblivious to the disparity, for his eyes warmed with pleasure at the sight of Priscilla's fresh, unpretentious beauty.

While Quint helped their young sister into his maroon

and yellow Stanhope pulled by the pretty sorrel mare, Jem helped the oldest and middle sisters into the gig pulled by the placid Comet. "Mind your fancy velvet," Madeline warned, sitting forward to protect her own Cambridge blue cloak. "There are a number of broken canes in the seat."

"Drat!" Bella muttered, sitting forward as her sister was doing.

"You need not come if you will be uncomfortable, Bella. I can still take Jem."

"Never mind about my comfort," she said, looking disdainfully at the placid Comet. "Just see if you can prod that dead horse into moving before Mr. Devon leaves us behind. Such a pretty animal."

Not for an instant did Madeline misinterpret the compliment as being meant for Comet, the old roan gelding who was already making his slow, cumbersome way down the driveway.

"Now," Madeline said, once the gig was safely in the lane, with Quint's pretty sorrel mare following close behind them, obviously champing at the bit to be allowed to move at a faster clip than Comet's snail pace. "Why did you come along, Bella? And do not try to fob me off with protestations of innocence, for I know you. You never do anything unless it benefits you in some way."

"You malign me," Bella replied. "I came merely to lend credence to our mother's scheme to get Mr. Devon to take our sister up in his handsome, and very expensive, sporting vehicle, thereby giving the chit another opportunity to attach him."

Madeline glanced at her sister to see if she was in earnest. Apparently she was. "Am I to infer that you have abandoned your plan to offer Priscilla to the nabob?" She could not bring herself to speak Philip's name, for fear she would lose her precarious hold on her emotions and burst into tears.

"That crow has been picked," she said testily, "and is now nothing but bones, so let us speak no more upon the subject. Our sister means to go her own way, no matter what devastation befalls the rest of us."

"So?" Madeline drawled.

"So, I decided to give my aid to this match with Devon. I would much prefer to speak of my brother-in-law, the baron's heir, than of my brother-in-law, the butcher's boy."

Madeline was hard-pressed not to laugh. "A wise choice. And?"

"And I realize now that I was on a fool's errand to think of pushing Priscilla to try her luck with Philip Balenger. But I was not thinking too clearly. Otherwise, I would have known that with his great wealth, our neighbor could look as high as he wishes for a bride. A lady with a title of her own is not out of the question, and the nabob must be aware of that fact. In all probability, he would laugh at the idea of aligning himself with a country miss, no matter how pretty her face and figure. And for my part, I have no wish to appear ridiculous before the world."

Madeline pressed her lips tightly shut and kept her gaze straight ahead, lest Bella discover how close her older sister had come to making a laughingstock of herself.

"So," Lady Townsend continued, "I have set my mind to fostering the attachment between our sister and Lord Holmes's heir. Perhaps his lordship is a generous man. If so, he might provide his son's bride with enough pin money to make it possible for her to help her family from time to time. And if not, at least she could invite

Townsend and me to Stavely. I would not mind being able to visit such a home whenever I chose."

Bella chattered on in this vein until the five-mile drive to Little Easton was accomplished. "Well," she said, "we seem to have made it to the village without mishap. One can only wonder, was it a result of Mr. Devon's escort, or was the gypsy lad's promise of doom an empty threat. For my part, I begin to believe it all a hum. Townsend might just as well have saved his money and not hired the Bow Street Runner.

Seeing no point in disabusing Bella of her fantasy at this late date, Madeline kept her thoughts to herself and gave Comet the office to turn right, then halt in front of the small two-story brick building that housed the establishments of the draper and the milliner. "I assume you would prefer to wait at Madame Jolie's while I go on to the Green Knight, where the carter is waiting."

"Oh, yes. You deliver your letters to your basket weavers. While you are gone, I shall entertain myself by trying on that pretty green bonnet in the window. Do you see the one I mean?" she asked, stepping down from the gig onto the sidewalk. "The one with the satin ruching and the wide, curling feather. Is it not enchanting?"

"Quite."

Instead of paying heed to what she was doing, Madeline gave her attention to the green bonnet, and as she leaned across the seat of the gig, she felt a tug, which was followed immediately by a ripping sound.

"Drat. I am caught on a broken cane."

Turning to survey the damage, Madeline discovered a large, gaping rent in the back of her cloak. "Blast and double blast!" she said, freeing the material. "It needed only this. It is not bad enough I am obliged to wear a mantle sadly out of fashion, now I shall appear the veriest ragamuffin into the bargain."

"No need to fall into a distempered freak," her sympathetic sister recommended. "You were a lackwit not to watch what you were about. But never mind that now. Here is the draper's boy come to take the horse. Climb down and come inside the shop; perhaps Madame Jolie can mend the thing. No point in sitting in the middle of the lane muttering to yourself like an old wigsby."

"Is aught amiss?" Priscilla asked as she and Mr. Devon drew alongside the gig.

"Maddy was so careless as to get caught on a broken cane, and now she is acting cross as crabs. But we are going inside Madame Jolie's to see what can be done to repair the torn material." Without petitioning Madeline's opinion on the subject, she added, "We do not need you, Priscilla. Why do you not take Mr. Devon across the street for a visit to the circulating library? You can rejoin us in half an hour."

The young lady and gentleman were more than agreeable to this scheme, so turning the Stanhope over to the draper's lad, they took themselves off without further ado, leaving Madeline and Bella to enter the milliner's shop alone.

At the tinkling of the little silver bell above the shop door, a middle-aged lady of improbably black hair and ruthlessly corseted girth came from behind a delicate, gilt desk to greet the sisters.

"*Mademoiselle*. M'lady," she said, her button brown eyes making a quick perusal of Bella's London finery. *Vraiment*, 'tis a pleasure to see you both."

"Madame," Bella said, pushing Madeline by the shoulder and turning her so the milliner could see the rip, "can you help us?"

"*Mais oui. Moi*, I shall have it mended within *ze* hour."

"An hour? But the carter is waiting for me at the hotel. I cannot—"

"You may wear my cloak," Bella offered in a rare show of generosity. "But for heaven's sake, do not let anything happen to it!"

Promising to guard the crimson velvet with her life, Madeline gave the blue into madame's keeping. Then, with infinite care, she slipped Bella's cloak around her shoulders and pulled the hood, with its lush white velvet lining, up over her hair.

"I shall return within a very few minutes," she said above the tinkling of the silver bell, "just as soon as I deliver the letters."

Closing the shop door behind her, Madeline realized the lad had taken the gig around to the rear of the buildings. However, after remembering the broken cane, she decided to walk rather than risk Bella's luxurious velvet. Her decision made, she strolled up the cobbled street toward the Green Knight Family Hotel.

She had only just passed the saddlery, and was crossing the alley between the saddler's and the confectioner's, when she was suddenly grabbed from behind by a veritable mountain of a man. His large, powerful arm snaked around her waist, jerking her roughly against his wide, barrel chest, and lifting her feet several inches off the ground. Before she could scream, the man clamped his beefy hand across her mouth.

Frightened nearly out of her wits, Madeline fought with all her strength. Kicking. Pushing. Trying to bite the hand that nearly smothered her. Unfortunately her protestations had little effect upon her captor, who paid scant attention to the war she waged. As though she were of no more significance than a captured hare, the kidnapper dragged her to the rear of the alley, where a coach and pair waited behind the saddlery.

"Ye were warned, missus," he muttered next to her ear. "Ignoring that warning were a mistake. And one ye'll learn to rue 'fore you be much older. This be the third day. Now ye must pay the price for your folly."

Chapter 13

Mr. Devon passed through the iron gates of Balenger Hall at a reckless pace that lifted the right wheel of his maroon and yellow Stanhope completely off the ground. Once the vehicle was on the carriageway, he prodded the pretty sorrel to even greater speed. At the portico, he yanked the lathered horse to a stop, then jumped to the ground.

"Philip!" he yelled as he pounded the heavy brass knocker. "Philip!"

Singh snatched the door open, his impassive face altered only by the slightest lifting of an eyebrow.

"Where is Mr. Balenger? I—" Mr. Devon stopped, for the nabob was already in the hallway, hurrying toward his friend.

"Ecod, man. What has happened?"

"She has been abducted!" he said, struggling to regain his breath, as though he, and not the mare, had galloped the four miles from the village.

"Who has been taken? Speak up, man! Who do you mean?"

Almost of its own volition, Philip's gaze went to the zigzag scar on his right hand, while a vivid memory flashed through his mind of the day he was attacked and dragged away by the press-gang. Along with that recollection came another—the gut-wrenching feeling of being overpowered. He had been a tall lad when he was impressed, and he had put up a fierce fight, giving almost as good as he got. But the gang had finally subdued him.

As Philip remembered those feelings of helplessness, and imagined how much more powerless a female must feel than a tall lad, something very like a rope squeezed painfully around his chest.

"It was Madeline," Mr. Devon answered. "They took Miss Wycliff."

The rope squeezed even tighter, threatening to burst Philip's heart and lungs, and he was forced to reach out and grasp the edge of a heavy console table to steady himself. "When?" he asked.

Mr. Devon had regained some control of his breathing. "Not more than half an hour ago."

Suddenly angry, Philip asked, "Where was that fool runner? I told him not to let Madeline out of his sight."

"He did not. Or, at least he thought he did not. When she came out of the millinery, Miss Wycliff was wearing her sister's cloak. The runner thought she was Lady Townsend. I have no doubt the kidnapper thought so as well."

"Damnation! Could the runner do nothing to stop the villain?"

"He tried. As soon as he saw Miss Wycliff being dragged into the alley, he ran to her defense. Only there must have been two villains, for someone cudgeled him from behind. To my regret, I was across the street, too far away to be of any assistance. Even though I ran to the alley with all possible speed, and continued to the coach, I arrived just as the driver set the horses to."

For the first time, Philip noticed his friend's torn coat sleeve and the handkerchief wrapped around the young man's hand. "Are you hurt?"

"Nothing to signify. I tried to wrench the coach door open. Unfortunately it was moving too fast. I was thrown to the ground."

"And the runner? Was he able to give pursuit?"

Mr. Devon shook his head. "He has a gash in his crown, and was still unable to stand when last I saw him. I paused for a moment to assure myself the man was not dead. Then I was obliged to force my way through a gathering crowd of gawkers in order to reach the high street."

"Go on, man."

"When I broke through the press, I found Miss Priscilla standing there in the street. She had obviously followed me across to the alley, and now her face was as white as my cravat. But she was pluck to the backbone," he added, pride in his voice. "No simpering miss, she had already instructed the draper's lad to retrieve the Wycliff gig and drive to the squire's to notify him of the kidnapping."

The young man squared his shoulders as if confessing a grievous error. "I am sorry, Philip. I had meant to jump in my carriage and follow the abductors, but by the time I ascertained where my mare had been taken, the coach carrying Miss Wycliff was already out of sight. And with me not knowing the area, I had no idea which way they had gone. Then I remembered that I . . . I had no weapon with me, and no more than a few pounds in my pocket. Should the villains' destination be any great distance, I had no funds to secure another horse. I thought the next best thing was to come for you."

Philip set his hand on the young man's shoulder. "You did all within your power, lad. You have nought to repine."

Wasting no more time, Philip instructed Singh to send word to the stable to have the Arab saddled and brought around. "As soon as that is accomplished, have a fresh horse put to Mr. Devon's Stanhope. I want two men to arm themselves, then accompany Mr. Devon's carriage back to the village to escort the Wycliff ladies home. The men are to remain at Wybourne to protect the ladies, but the runner who is there at present is to be sent on to me. I may have need of a man of his special talents."

"It shall be done, sahib."

As Singh sped to carry out his instructions, Philip hurried to the book room, Mr. Devon following just behind him. Going straight to the massive desk, Philip opened the top drawer and removed a pistol. After making certain the weapon was loaded, he slipped it into the inside pocket of his coat.

Lastly he withdrew a leather envelope from the same drawer, extracted a large stack of pound notes from the pouch, then stuffed the money inside another pocket. "Just in case," he said.

When the two gentlemen returned to the foyer, Singh stood beside the open door, Philip's driving coat, hat, and gloves at hand.

Hearing the Arab's hoofbeats on the driveway, Philip shrugged into the coat, set his hat on his head, then hurried outside and swung up into the saddle. Without a backward glance, he turned the powerful horse toward the entrance gates and galloped away.

Scarcely an hour after being dragged down the alley, thrown into a foul-smelling, poorly sprung coach, and transported to heaven-knew-where, Madeline found herself being hauled out of the vehicle. They had stopped in a long-deserted field, and once she was out in the fresh air, she had breathed deeply, hoping to rid her nose of the stench of the sour hay on the floor of the coach and the fetid breath of the man who held her roughly by the wrists. Unfortunately her time out of doors was short, for the kidnapper slung her over his shoulder, like a bag of oats, then carried her across the field to a cottage that was little better than a hut.

The mud building was old, probably built by crofters a good two centuries ago, and its yellow wash had faded and was now covered by decades of dirt and grime. The man did not pause in the single, all-purpose room that comprised the whole of the downstairs, but immediately climbed a crude ladder to a small, dimly lit sleeping loft where he dumped Madeline, like so much refuse, onto a filthy bed.

Without uttering a word, her porter turned and left the room, slamming the door behind him.

Now Madeline sat on the bed with its clammy, moth-eaten coverlet, her back propped against one of the rough-hewn oak bedposts. She had drawn her legs up to her chest, then wrapped her sister's velvet cloak around her for warmth and whatever protection it might afford.

The bed took up most of the space in the tiny loft, leaving little room for walking around. Not that Madeline had any intention of setting so much as a foot on that floor—not until she had to—for when the brute who carried her up the ladder had shoved open the door, dozens of mice had scurried out of his way.

Of course, mice were the least of Madeline's worries. She was far too frightened of the two-legged rats who had brought her to this long-deserted cottage to worry overmuch about the little furry creatures.

She was especially afraid of the large brute who had done all the dragging and hauling. She had reason to be. After pitching her into the coach, he had climbed in after her and forced her face to the disgusting floor. "Keep down," he ordered, putting his large booted foot on her neck. "If ye move, or make a noise, I'll kill ye right here

and now. One good push be all it 'ud need. Y'er lily-
white neck 'ud snap like a twig."

Madeline had kept to the floor, in no doubt of the
man's sincerity, but that *Kill ye right here and now* had
gnawed at her brain, sending shivers of fear through her
body. The sentence sounded as though part of it had
been left unsaid, the frightening conclusion being, *as op-
posed to later*.

Adding to her present anxiety was the fact that the
three kidnappers had made no effort to disguise their
faces. It being daylight, Madeline had seen the men
clearly and could easily identify each of them. She had
even heard them call one another by name.

The gargantuan was called Dolph, while his accom-
plices answered to Penn and Zeb. One of them had even
mentioned getting word to someone called Mr. Flynn.
Their careless disregard for her ability to give testimony
against them later, and help bring them to justice, boded
ill for Madeline's chances of ever leaving the cottage
alive.

But leave it she would! Even if she died in the attempt. Far better to die trying, than to go passively, like
a sheep at slaughter time—resigned and unresisting.

Madeline had made herself a promise while still in the
coach, crouched on the floor like an animal with the
lout's foot on her neck. She had felt her tears spilling
onto her folded arms, and at that moment she had made a
bargain with herself. *If you will be strong,* she promised
the terrified person inside her, *and not give in to fear and
despair, I will get you out of this mess.*

The warm tears spilling across her forearm had reminded Madeline of the zigzag scar Philip wore as a re-
minder of his kidnapping. When he had been abducted
by the press-gang, Philip had been much younger than
she—little more than a boy—with neither the knowledge

nor the mental fortitude that comes to a person through years of experience. Madeline was five and twenty, a woman of intelligence and inner strength. If a boy could endure years of cruel enslavement aboard ship, she could survive whatever lay in store for her.

And, she remembered with a reviving of her spirit, Philip had finally fled his captors. He had escaped in a foreign land, with no one to call upon for help, and no one to run to once he was free. The same was not true of Madeline. She was not so very far from home, and if her absence was not already remarked, very soon her family would be looking for her.

She had only to keep to her personal bargain.

In order to devise a plan of escape, Madeline tried to remember all the sights, sounds, and impressions she had experienced since being hauled from the coach. The drive has lasted about an hour, but she was not concerned at the present over where the cottage was located. All she wanted was to be out of it. She would worry about finding her way home after she escaped the kidnappers.

It was the layout of the cottage that concerned her for the moment. Earlier she had noted that her prison consisted of nothing more than the ground-floor room and the sleeping loft, with a front door, two windows—one to the front, one to the side—and a small, low dormer window just beneath the high-pitched, thatched roof.

Since the kidnappers sat belowstairs, enjoying the fire whose smoke Madeline smelled through the uncaulked floorboards, she knew, without needing to ponder the question overlong, that sneaking through the front door was out of the question. Therefore, if she was to escape, it would have to be through the dormer.

Because Dolph was such a large man, it had probably never occurred to him that anyone might possibly fit through the small window; otherwise, he would have bound Madeline's hands and feet. But she was slender, and she meant to do everything in her power to squeeze through that aperture.

She could do nothing, however, until it grew dark. Under the cover of darkness, she meant to climb out the window, get as far away from the cottage as possible, then find a good place to hide until it was safe to make her way back to Little Easton and home.

Madeline might not be focusing her concern on the actual location of the cottage, but the matter was of paramount interest to Philip. And while she eagerly awaited the arrival of darkness, he begged heaven to stay the sun until he found her. The coach might have left the lane at any place, and once night fell, it would be impossible to follow the wheel tracks. As well, there was a smell of rain in the air, and if the search was delayed until tomorrow, the tracks might be washed away.

One gigantic piece of good fortune had already been granted him—that of discovering which lane the coach had taken after leaving the main road. Without that bit of luck, he might even now be galloping into the town of Glastonbury, the real trail lost.

After questioning several members of the crowd that still gathered around the alley where the kidnapping had taken place, and ascertaining that the coach had passed the Green Knight, then veered left, taking the main road south, to Glastonbury, Philip had urged the Arab in that direction. Half an hour later, as the horse galloped down the road, some propitious spirit led Philip to glance to his right, down a small lane. There, standing in a field of tall grass mixed with wild foxglove, was the Wycliff gig, manned by a lad of about twelve years.

Recalling Quint's words, that Miss Priscilla had sent

the draper's boy to fetch the squire, Philip would have ridden on by had the lad not waved his arms above his head, his manner quite excited. "Sir!" he yelled. "Stop!"

Reining in the Arab, Philip turned him down the lane, then approached the boy in the gig. Today, the slug of a horse that had once shied and left Madeline stranded did not even flinch at their arrival, so intent was he upon eating his fill of the wild grass.

"Sir," the boy began, jumping from the gig and running toward Philip. "They turned up this lane. That be their tracks just there." He pointed to a slight indentation in the grass. "They be faint, but that be them, right and tight."

"What is this? Were you not sent to fetch the squire?"

The boy lowered his gaze. "Yes, sir. But I saw the coach take the south road, and I decided it would serve Miss Wycliff better if I was to follow. And right I was, for it turned off here."

His youthful mouth pulled down in a look of disgust. "Not that I saw it with my own eyes, mind you—this horse being no better than a milch cow at moving. But I followed the wheel tracks—plain as a pikestaff they was—till suddenly they disappeared from the road. I got down to have a better look, and sure as Bob's your uncle, there they were, clear as day, turning onto this lane. See where the grass is crushed just along to the right?"

Philip dismounted, and holding on to the Arab's reins, he let the lad show him the tracks on the road and the point at which they turned onto the lane. "Good boy," he said, encouraged by this solid clue to the abductors' direction.

Reaching into his coat pocket, Philip found a gold sovereign, which he placed in the boy's hand. "I want you to go back to the village and tell some responsible adult what you discovered. Tell them I have followed the tracks, but that I may need help. If you should see a large, yellow-haired man wearing a red vest, be certain to tell him the whole, for he is a Bow Street Runner in my hire."

"Cooee!" the boy said, forcing his attention from the guinea in his hand. "A runner. Fancy that."

Philip waited only long enough to make certain the lad got the lazy gelding out of the grass and back on the road before he began the process of following the coach tracks. The task, though of necessity slow, was not too difficult, mainly because the wide coach had been obliged to stay out of the heavily wooded areas to either side of the lane. As a result, Philip spotted the vehicle within a short time. It stood in what must once have been a farmer's field, but was now nothing more than rough land and gorse.

Smelling smoke and guessing that a house of some sort lay beyond the hedgerow in the distance, Philip turned the Arab to the opposite side of the lane where a stand of trees offered shelter from prying eyes and the rain, which would come soon, judging from the distant rumble of thunder. The reins securely tied around a low limb, Philip left the horse, crossed the lane, then cautiously approached the coach.

The vehicle was empty, of course, but the smell of smoke had grown stronger, so Philip followed the aroma to the other side of the hedgerow, where he spied a crofter's cottage. The ancient dwelling was only slightly larger than a hut, and round—with no corners in which the devil could hide, or so the old-timers believed—and it had an unlived-in look, the smoke spiraling from the chimney notwithstanding.

The presence of the two thick-bodied coach horses that were tied to a tree on the far side of the cottage told

Philip he had come to the right place. He had found the malefactors. Now he must find Madeline. And God help the kidnappers if they had hurt her in any way!

Keeping close to the hedgerow, Philip circled the decaying structure. It boasted only one door and two ground-floor windows, but beneath the eaves of the thatched roof was a small dormer, attesting to the existence of an upper room. The window was about twelve feet from the ground, so looking inside was out of the question, but if Madeline was in the cottage, Philip would wager she was in that upper room.

He was debating the advisability of sneaking up to one of the lower windows to see how many people might be inside, when a loud clap of thunder sounded, startling the horses and causing them to neigh and move about. The door was thrown open, and Philip ducked behind the hedgerow just as two men came outside, their pistols drawn.

Strangers to the area, they were the kind of ruffians all too common in the city, their clothes ill fitting and far from new, and their faces aged prematurely by poverty and rum. While Philip watched them approach the horses, a third man appeared in the doorway.

It was the ex-pugilist Philip had seen in the public room of the Green Knight. The tapster had pointed out the unfriendly stranger with the overly developed upper body, the broken nose, and the thick neck. Standing there in the doorway, his coarse coat discarded and his shirtsleeves rolled up to his elbows, the man looked even larger and more dangerous than he had appeared in the tavern.

"Quit y'er dawdling," he ordered, "and get them horses 'fore they bolt. Lest ye wish to walk back to Lunnon."

Whatever the other two replied, it was lost in the thunder that seemed to roll from a far distance, gathering quickly then booming so loudly it shook the ground beneath Philip's feet.

The large man stepped back from the doorway as the other two came running, each tugging at a nervous horse. While Philip watched, both men and animals disappeared inside the cottage. The door shut behind them just as another clap of thunder sounded.

At least the question had been answered as to how many men were inside. Three men, at least two of them armed, and the third in no need of a weapon. Even with a pistol in his pocket, Philip was not fool enough to believe he could overtake three men. Therefore, two possibilities remained. He could stay where he was and wait for reinforcements to arrive, or he could see if there was a way to reach that dormer window without being detected.

He decided on the latter, chiefly because the clouds were darkening the sky and large raindrops had begun to fall. Bad weather would keep help from arriving. If the rains came as fast and hard as the thunder, not only would it be difficult to follow the tracks, but it also would be impossible to travel, for the lane would turn into a quagmire.

Madeline heard the thunder, then the neighing of the horses and the sound of men running about outside. When she heard Dolph yell, she left the bed and went over to the dormer to see what was happening. The window being only a foot or so above the floor, she had to bend way down to see out.

She had been waiting for the cover of night, but now she saw that she could wait no longer. With the coming of the storm, the light was fading sooner than she had anticipated. If she did not hurry, the room would be in total darkness, and she would be unable to see what she was about. Time now a factor, Madeline removed the cloak from her shoulders and threw it onto the bed. With all haste, she began to unbutton her dress.

In a matter of seconds, the rose chambray fell to her ankles. The dress was followed by her white lawn petticoat. Next she untied the little roll bustle from around her waist. After loosening and discarding her stays, she was left with nothing covering her but her short-sleeved chemise and her drawers, and the bone-chilling air seemed to go through that scant covering right to her skin, making her teeth rattle with the cold.

"Just get on with it," she mumbled, "or you will find yourself cold in your grave."

Her resolve reinforced by that happy prediction, Madeline pulled the filthy coverlet toward her and began stuffing it into her dress, molding the bulk into what she hoped would resemble a sleeping form. The dress filled, she turned it on its side, with the back facing the door; then she spread the hem so the end of the skirt appeared to be covering the sleeper's feet. For the head, she wound her bustle roll into her petticoat and stuffed it inside the collar of the dress.

If Dolph came to check on her, especially if he did not bring a strong light, he might be fooled by the stuffed dress. The deception would give her added time to make her escape.

The substitution completed, Madeline hurried back to the dormer. Unfortunately this part of her plan proved more difficult than she had imagined. The small-paned window was held fast by decades of grime, and difficult to lift, screeching in protest each time she tried to pull it open. She was obliged to wait for claps of thunder to cover the noise. After what seemed like years, the frame finally gave way, and Madeline was able to yank it free and hook the pull in the ceiling bracket.

Tiptoeing across the room, she waited for a clap of thunder. Then she eased the door open far enough to see if all three men were inside the cottage. They were. Satisfied that the time had come, she waited for more thunder before closing the door.

After taking a deep breath to steady her shaky nerves, she rolled her sister's cloak into a ball, then threw it out the window.

When no one yelled or came running to investigate the flying velvet, Madeline got down on her hands and knees, with her head toward the door. Slowly, carefully she slipped her right leg through the window, stopping when her kneecap touched the threshold. Then she slipped her left leg in beside the right. With most of her weight on her hands, she backed through the window, inch by painstaking inch, until her legs stuck straight out into space.

Cold raindrops beat down on her legs and backside, quickly soaking her thin drawers and turning them into an icy film, making maneuvering even more difficult.

For one awful moment, Madeline thought her hips had become stuck in the opening. Working them loose took a good deal of squirming and breath holding, but finally she pushed free. She was out to her waist, dangling half in, half out of the window, the threshold nearly cutting her in two.

Now came the tricky part—truly Hobson's choice. She could either climb down or fall down.

Hoping desperately for the former, Madeline slid the toe of her boot along the outside wall as much as she dared, looking for a foothold. When she found no breaks in the smooth, mud structure, a combination of anger and self-pity threatened what little calm she possessed.

She wanted to scream at the fates. All around her the cottage was falling apart with rot; there were holes and fissures every place except where she needed one. Beneath the spot where she climbed out, the wall was still intact!

Since climbing down was out of the question, that left only choice number two—falling. Of course, she would try to hang by her arms, then drop to the ground, but she had little faith in her ability to do so.

Committed now, come what may, Madeline raised her right arm and eased it between her ribs and the jamb, placing her hand on the threshold. Repeating the process with her left arm, she teetered dangerously and was obliged to grip the threshold with all her strength. Forced to delay a moment while her heart moved out of her throat and back into her chest, she was at last ready to make the final move, which meant pushing up on her hands just far enough to allow her bust through the aperture.

Gritting her teeth against the possibility of losing her grip and hurtling through space, perhaps breaking something when she hit the ground, she said a quick prayer and then pushed with all her might. To her surprise, she did not slide. In fact, she barely moved. Something—or someone—was pushing against the soles of her boots.

Chapter 14

Philip had been waiting for the right degree of darkness to try his hand at climbing up the smooth outer wall of the cottage to see if Madeline was, indeed, being held in the upper room. That moment had arrived. Another few minutes and the dark that shielded him from view would also make it impossible for him to see. As well, the rain threatened to make climbing a very tricky affair.

Standing beneath the small window of that room, intent upon his search for cracks or holes in the surface that would provide him with toeholds, Philip was startled into muttering a curse when a missile of some kind sailed through the air. As he watched, the object opened up and floated soundlessly to the ground.

Instantly his hand went to the pistol in his coat pocket. Pulling the hammer back in readiness, he crept over to the mysterious object and touched it with his boot. It was a woman's cloak.

What idiocy was this? Why would anyone toss a cloak out? And to what purpose?

He found the next item of clothing to emerge from the window even more astonishing, for it was a pair of women's drawers. And quite amazingly, the woman was still in them.

Damnation!

Realizing what was happening—that Madeline was

attempting to escape by climbing out the window—
Philip was torn between two emotions: fear that she
would fall and seriously injure herself, and admiration
for her bravery.

Of course, he was unable to understand why she
thought it necessary to take her clothes off, but he put
that question aside in deference to the more important
consideration of how he was to assist her without frightening her out of her wits. If he startled her, she might
fall, or at the very least cry out. Either way, the kidnappers would be alerted to the fact that she was escaping.

Holding his breath, and willing her to move cautiously, Philip watched helplessly as Madeline inched
her way through the dormer. When she remained mo-
tionless for a couple of minutes, his heart nearly stopped.
He was terrified that she might be stuck in the small
opening. However, to his great relief, she soon began to
move again. When she was halfway out the window, she
tried to find a toehold in the smooth wall, but from the
frantic way her boot moved back and forth, he knew she
was having no success.

As Philip watched her ease her hands onto the threshold, he saw the unsteadiness of the movement and knew
that she hadn't the strength in her arms needed to push
out, then hang for a drop to the ground. Whatever she
had planned, the truth of the matter was that without
help, she was doomed to a nasty fall.

Unable to think of an alternative, he reached up and
set his palms under the soles of her boots, pushing up-
ward just enough to let her know there was someone beneath her, offering her a bit of support.

"I am here," he whispered. "Do not let go just yet. See
if you can hang on long enough to allow me to—"

" 'Ere, what's this?" a gruff voice inside yelled.

Philip saw an angry face appear at the front window.

Then he heard a curse. "Devil take it! The wench be escaping."

"Drop, Maddy! Now!"

Whether Madeline dropped or fell, she did not know, but whichever it was, she was caught by the one man she had thought never to see again.

She felt Philip stagger momentarily from the impact of her body crashing into his. Somehow he managed to keep his balance. And though her heart pounded fit to break through her chest—a combination of joy at Philip's being there and fear at the risk he was taking—he allowed her no time to voice either of those feelings. The moment he was steady on his feet, he set her down, gave her a push between her shoulder blades, and ordered her to run.

Madeline obeyed, but she had taken no more than a half dozen steps when she heard Dolph's voice. "Halt," he yelled, "or I'll shoot!"

An instant later, an explosion rent the air, causing her heart to stop beating. "Philip!" she screamed.

"I told you to go," he said angrily, very close to her ear.

"I thought—"

"Do not think. Run."

Philip grabbed her by the upper arm, then half propelled, half dragged her into a wood off to the right of the cottage.

She heard a second report of gunfire, but by that time they were out of range—or so Philip assured her. "We must keep going," he said. "That first shot came from my pistol, so I am now without a weapon."

They ran for a very long time—hours, it seemed to Madeline—before Philip said they might stop and rest a few minutes. "As soon as you have caught your breath," he said, his own breathing almost as ragged as hers, "we will double back and see if we can make it to my horse. I think we lost our pursuers. They are city men, and have not our advantage of familiarity with the wooded terrain."

The rain had lessened considerably, but Madeline was already drenched to the skin. Now that they had stopped running, she began to shiver, her teeth chattering like Spanish castanets.

"May I have my cloak?"

The darkness had reduced everything to obsidian shapes, but she could tell that Philip was removing his greatcoat. Somewhat awkwardly, he pulled his arms free of the sleeves, then draped the coat around her shoulders.

The sudden warmth of the soft wool was indescribably comforting, while the almost imperceptible aroma that clung to the fabric—a masculine smell Madeline would have known anywhere as belonging to Philip—was most disturbing to her peace of mind. She hugged the coat close to her body, though whether her aim was to savor the warmth, or the essence of Philip, she could not say.

"There was no time to retrieve the cloak," he said. "I am sorry."

"No, please. You owe me no apology. Not for anything. I . . . I cannot tell you how grateful I was just to hear your voice. Only minutes before, I had been so frightened. I have never felt so alone in my life, and so . . .." She stopped. Another word and she would burst into tears.

"I know," he said softly.

"Yes. I know you do. Remembering your survival helped me withstand my own gnawing fear. Just thinking of you helped."

Unable to stay her hand, Madeline reached up and touched Philip's face, letting her fingertips trace the firm, angular jaw of the man she loved. His flesh felt warm against her cold skin. His lips felt even warmer when he turned his head and burned a kiss into her palm.

It was all she could do not to throw herself into his arms. She ached to feel those warm lips upon her mouth. She wanted desperately to wrap her arms around his waist and press her face into his comforting shoulder, to feel his answering strength. Hopefully, longingly she waited for her buccaneer to enfold her in his powerful embrace.

When he made no move to touch her, Madeline finally dropped her hand from his face and stepped back.

She had forgotten. He was not *her* buccaneer. He was not her anything. Never had been. That flight of fancy had been no more than self-delusion. He was Philip Balenger. The nabob. And whatever had led him to this deserted place just when she needed him most, it had nothing to do with his wanting to hold her in his arms.

Resigned to the fact that any warmth she received must come from the greatcoat, Madeline slipped first one arm then the other into the sleeves, and as she did so, she noticed that the left sleeve felt especially rough against her bare skin. When she reached up to investigate the roughness, her probing fingers discovered a large, ragged hole in the wool.

While her mind sought desperately to refute the origin of the hole, and to deny the throat-clutching realization that Philip must have a corresponding wound in his upper arm, the dark shape standing before her began to sway.

"Philip," she cried, reaching out to steady him as he slumped against her. "You have been shot."

"You should have told me," Madeline scolded gently, pulling the greatcoat up closer around their shoulders.

"All that running, and you never said a word. You must have lost a great deal of blood."

" 'Tis but a scratch," he whispered, giving himself up to a not unpleasant floating sensation. Though, in all honesty, Philip could not say whether his condition owed more to the blood he had lost, or the fact that Madeline was lying beside him, her head on his shoulder and her nearly naked body pressed against his—to keep him warm, she said.

Somehow she had found a makeshift shelter—a bower, she had called it—consisting of a tangled thicket of low-hanging boughs, bramble bushes, and stinging nettle. And though he had wanted to keep on running, to get as far away from the kidnappers as possible, he had given in to her pleas and agreed to crawl inside the hideaway until help arrived. If his amenable disposition had more to do with a weakness in the knees than to any keenness of perception on his part, his lovely mermaid was charitable enough to ignore the lapse, choosing instead to bestow upon him both her sympathy and her sweet, delectable person.

"Be still," he whispered hoarsely when she snuggled closer, her soft breasts pressing against his ribs in a manner guaranteed to set him aflame from head to foot.

"Did I hurt you?" she asked solicitously.

"My arm is fine. Just do not move anymore. Please. Unless you wish to be obliged to defend your virtue, you would do well to remember that I am merely wounded, not dead."

"Oh," she said softly.

"Oh, indeed. Just have a care, little mermaid, for I am but flesh and blood."

"Yes, but less blood than usual," she reminded him. "And in your present, debilitated state, I believe I could mill you down if need be."

Madeline felt, rather than heard, his chuckle, for it vibrated in his chest, sending tingling sensations through her body.

"If I were you," he said, "I would not wager any large sums of money upon your ability to subdue the beast in me. Especially when you will keep dousing yourself with water—a thing you would not do if you knew what it does to me. Or what I wish to do to you."

"What do you wish?" she asked saucily. "To make me walk the plank in retribution for getting you shot? Or, perhaps you are tired of rescuing me and wish to toss me into the sea, once and for all?"

"Do not wager even a groat on that absurdity. What I want to do to you, my enchantress, is take you in my arms and kiss you until you promise to forsake your sea home forever and sail away with me."

Though her heart nearly stopped at his lover-like words, Madeline had learned to her sorrow not to take Philip's jests too seriously, for they were but a part of his unconventional manners. She knew he did not *really* want her to sail away with him; it was just his way. On the other hand, he had said he wanted to take her in his arms and kiss her, and she wanted that very thing so much she ached from the wanting.

"I know you are merely funning me, Philip. But if you would not dislike it too much, I . . ." The actual voicing of her wish was so difficult Madeline very nearly cried craven. Taking a deep breath, she said it all in a rush. "I should like very much to be kissed."

Philip lay very still, so still Madeline feared he might have fallen asleep. However, she soon learned that he was very much awake, when his right arm, the arm that had thus far rested companionably around her shoulders, moved ever so slowly to her waist, trailing tingles of warmth down her spine.

He clasped her quite firmly, surprisingly so for a man she had thought of as weakened by a debilitating injury, and drew her body across his chest, settling her so their faces were mere inches apart. His warm breath teased a wisp of hair that had fallen across her cheek.

She could not see his mouth, but seeing it was not necessary. So strong was the magnetism of his lips, that it pulled her closer, ever closer, until at last their lips touched.

The kiss was soft at first, the contact light. A gentle, feathery meeting that sent rivulets of warmth flowing throughout every inch of her body. But after a few moments, Philip increased the pressure of his mouth, and gentle warmth soon became searing heat. His touch filled her with wonder, turning her bones to a molten substance whose singular purpose seemed to be to allow her pliable softness to be molded to his muscular hardness. Her senses awhirl, Madeline opened her lips in joyous response to Philip's demanding passion.

With a fluidity of motion that left her breathless, Philip took command of the embrace, switching their positions so that she was beneath him. With the weight of his body pressed against hers, she reveled in a heady, new sensation. Conscious of his strength, yet aware that he held it in check—for her sake—she felt empowered, liberated to do what she wished with him.

Her hands free now, Madeline slipped her fingers through his crisp hair, imagining as she did so that she could actually feel the warmth of the sun-streaked locks. When she slid her arms around his neck and gave a gentle tug, Philip knew exactly what she wanted, and he covered her eager mouth with his.

Madeline floated upon an ocean of delight, with wave after wave lifting her higher and higher until she thought she would drown, to die happily in the storm of Philip's passionate kisses. But even as she clung to him like a lifeline, he lifted his mouth from hers and drew away, leaving her feeling suddenly adrift.

"Madeline," he whispered, his voice so raspy she barely recognized it.

She tried to draw him to her, to reclaim his lips, but he rolled away, lying on his back once again. When she ventured to turn toward him, his right hand held her shoulder so that she was obliged to remain still. "Philip, please, let me—"

"Remain where you are," he muttered, his breathing ragged. "You've had enough kissing for one day. More than enough."

Bewildered by his rejection, she said, "But I thought . . ." That was the problem, of course, she had not thought. Once again she had merely reacted to being with him. It had felt so right, so natural—at least, it had seemed so to her. And now she feared her abandoned behavior had given Philip a disgust of her.

Madeline wanted to hide her face in shame. "I am sorry." Though she strove for a normal tone, her voice caught suspiciously, betraying the tears that stung her eyes. "I would not have forced myself upon you had I not thought you were enjoying it, too. I—"

"For the love of heaven, Madeline! You did n—"

"Hollo!" came a distant call. "Miss Wycliff. Mr. Balenger. Do ye hear me? All's well, and we be come to take you home."

"Shh! Do not answer," Philip cautioned, his words a whisper. "It could be a trick."

"But I know that voice. It belongs to Abel Frome, one of the cottagers. You bought a basket from his father, Willem Frome."

"Hollo, Philip!" came a second voice.

Madeline heard Philip's quick intake of breath. "It is Quint."

"Philip," Mr. Devon called again. "Can you hear me?"

Madeline would have crawled out of the bower on the instant to let the rescuers know the location of their hiding place, had Philip not caught her by the arm, stopping her. "Wait," he said, feeling around for the coat that had been pushed aside and forgotten in the heat of their kisses. When he found it, he handed it to her. "Put this on and button it all the way," he said quietly. "I would not have you embarrassed by gawking eyes."

Chapter 15

Madeline awoke in her own bed, surprised to find the early afternoon sun streaming through the window, the sun's rays revealing the rather ordinary room, with its walls washed in peach, its plain dressing table, its sturdy oak clothespress, and the commonplace washbowl and pitcher. Scarcely twenty hours had passed since she had prayed fervently to be returned to this bedchamber. But that entreaty had been sent heavenward before she shared the bower with Philip—before the short, wonderful time spent in the arms of the man she loved.

Now the familiarity of these homely surroundings did nothing to assuage the overpowering pain in Madeline's heart.

Philip had held her and kissed her, and she had responded, giving him her heart as well as her lips. She had felt the fires of passion and asked for nothing more than to spend eternity in her beloved's embrace. But the man she loved had not shared that wish. He had pushed her away. The fires of passion had become ashes, and here she was, once again in her own bed, alone.

Philip had said nothing to her after she crawled out of the small hiding place and yelled to the rescuers. Of course, everyone was talking at once—asking questions, telling her of the confrontation with the kidnappers and the hunt through the woods for her and Philip—but they would have hushed if Philip had spoken.

He did not.

He pretended to be unconscious, allowing the dozen or so hoe-wielding basket weavers to believe his state resulted from the bullet wound to his arm. And though Madeline knew this ploy was meant to safeguard her reputation, she had hoped for a word, a sign from him that she had somehow misunderstood his motive for pushing her away.

Philip had uttered no such word. He had given no such sign.

A knock at her bedroom door interrupted these unhappy recollections. "Maddy," Priscilla called, "may I come in?"

Not waiting for a reply to her request, the impetuous young lady pushed open the door and stepped inside the room, followed by Tess, who carried a small pewter tray on which reposed a pot of steaming chocolate and a plate of Mrs. Jinks's scones.

"You really do need to get up if you feel you can, Maddy," Priscilla said, planting a kiss on her sister's cheek, "for we have already been to church and returned, and now some of the cottagers have called to see how you fared your ordeal. They have been waiting outside for an hour or more."

"Outside! Why did you not invite them in? Surely my mother and Bella did not object to receiving them. Or even if they did, could you not have taken the visitors to the back parlor?"

Priscilla shook her head. "Your well-wishers would not fit into that small room. There are too many of them."

"Oh, miss," the maid said, stepping forward to set the tray across Madeline's knees and stack pillows behind her back, "there must be twenty-five or thirty people outside, all come to see how you get on."

Madeline looked past the maid to her sister, who nodded her head in agreement. "At least that many. And the basket weavers are not your only visitors. Quint was here earlier, as were a number of neighbors. Also, several floral offerings have arrived, and numerous messages."

Messages. Madeline's heart pounded in her chest. "Was there a message from Philip?" Seeing the interested look in the maid's eyes, Madeline forced her voice to a degree of calmness. "What I mean to say is, has anyone heard how Mr. Balenger is fairing? He was shot, you know, while helping me escape."

"We all know of his bravery," Priscilla answered quickly, "and I assure you, the entire family is cognizant of the debt we owe him. When mother sent a note around to inquire after the nabob's health, Quint rode over to give us the latest report."

"And he is well?"

"Yes. The doctor saw to the bullet wound last evening and pronounced it a fortuitous hit, with no real damage done. And you will be happy to know that the hero left his bed this morning and partook of a hearty breakfast. He is even now on the mend."

"Oh. I am pleased to hear of his recovery."

Thinking she needed to demonstrate her lack of distress at the knowledge that Philip had made no inquiry concerning her own well-being, Madeline nibbled an infinitesimal bite from one of the scones, only to discover that even so small a morsel balked at passing the aching lump in her throat. Taking a few moments to gain control of her emotions, she said, "I suppose I should send Mr. Balenger a letter expressing my gratitude for his rescue."

If her young sister heard the strain in Madeline's voice, she chose not to comment upon it. "Time enough for that later, Maddy. At the present, we have other matters to discuss. The first being, what do you wish to do about the cottagers? If you like, I can take down a message."

"I shall dress and go down to thank them for their concern." Giving her attention to Tess, she said, "Do you suppose Jinksie could provide some refreshments? Perhaps coffee and some of these scones?"

"Mrs. Jinks said as how you would be wanting refreshments, so she told Jem to set up a table in the side garden. Meanwhile, her and Maeve be fixing trays right now. There be heaping plates of hot scones, bread and butter, and orange marmalade, plus biscuits and milk for the children. Even the wee ones came, wishful to see for themselves that you had come to no harm."

The maid sighed romantically. "Only think of you being captured and then rescued, Miss Maddy. Just like the heroine in that book of Miss Priscilla's, the one about the wicked count. 'Course it weren't no count what kidnapped you, only them three scoundrels as was caught by the two Bow Street Runners. And if you was to ask me, it's a good thing that trio is being transported to London for trial, else folks here about might be tempted to show them what we think of villains who kidnap ladies off the streets of Little Easton."

"Happily," Priscilla said, interrupting this impassioned speech, "the abductors are even now on their way to jail, and the man responsible for hiring them to do his bidding will soon be apprehended. We can put this incident behind us."

"Yes, miss." Evident in the maid's voice was her disappointment that such interesting goings-on had to end. "But while it lasted, it was an adventure, fair enough!"

"That it was," Madeline replied, wanting to bring the conversation to an end. "Thank you for your concern, Tess. Now, if you will be so kind, please tell Jinksie that I approve her choice of refreshments, and that I shall be down in a few minutes."

Bobbing a curtsy, the maid replied a polite, "Yes, Miss Maddy," then hurried from the room.

Priscilla closed the door behind Tess, then returned to sit on the edge of her sister's bed. "Last night I promised I would not plague you with questions about what happened, and I mean to keep my promise—I will ask no questions, not even one. But I need to warn you about something Mama has made up her mind to do."

"Warn?" Madeline sighed. "Please tell me you used that word in error. Or that you mean only to inform me that Mama has decided to abandon her palpitations for a malady more au courant."

"If only it were that simple. Unfortunately that is not the case. I was not being completely honest when I told Tess we could now put the kidnapping incident behind us."

Madeline leaned back against the pillows the maid had seen fit to stack behind her. Closing her eyes, she said, "Please, Priscilla, if I must hear news of a distressing nature, let me have it plainly, and with no round-aboutation."

"It shall be as you wish. The matter concerns the fact that you arrived home wearing Philip's greatcoat, and little else. Mama and Bella were closeted together until late last night, then again this morning; the object of their discussion was the state of your *deshabille*. 'Shocking nakedness,' Bella called it. And now our sister has convinced Mama that you were compromised."

Groaning, Madeline inquired, "Compromised by whom? The kidnappers?"

Priscilla shook her head, her fair curls bouncing with the agitated movement. "Unless your wits have gone lacking, Maddy, you should know better than that. The kidnappers are not wealthy."

"Blast and double blast!"

"Exactly. Mama means to send Papa over to Balenger Hall the minute he returns. I do not suppose I need tell you what his mission will be."

"You do not."

Pushing the breakfast tray aside, Madeline threw the covers back and arose. In hopes of relieving a measure of her anger, she began to pace the floor of her bedchamber. "So this is how they would repay Philip for helping me escape almost certain death. By imposing marriage upon him."

Very quietly Priscilla asked, "Are you so certain Philip would find it an imposition?"

"Anyone must!"

"And what of you, Maddy? Forgive me for speaking upon a situation that I am certain you will say is none of my concern, but I have observed the way you look at him. I had thought I perceived a degree of attachment that—"

"No! You are mistaken. I find Philip amusing, that is true enough, but as for any warmer feelings, there are none. Not on my part. And certainly not on his."

"I think it is you who are mistaken, Maddy. He—"

"There is no point in our discussing the matter further. Philip and I would not suit, and there is an end to the subject. But I thank you for the warning. Of course, there is no need to tell me at whose door I may lay this idea of a forced marriage. It is but another of Bella's harebrained notions, another of our sister's schemes to become related to the nabob. And I will not have it!"

"What mean you to do?"

"At the moment, I plan to get dressed and go out to the side garden, to thank my well-wishers for their concern. After that, I shall inform Bella and our mother that I have no intention of marrying Philip Balenger." Her voice quivered just the tiniest fraction. "Not now. Not ever."

A full two hours had passed before the last of the cottagers had exchanged a few words with Madeline, had partaken of the refreshments, then said their good-byes. Madeline's intention of seeking Bella, to correct her sister's belief that the nabob's purse would soon be at her disposal, was denied by the sudden and unexpected arrival of Lord Townsend's traveling coach.

Madeline had just turned the corner of the house when a pair of lathered horses sped up the driveway. She recognized the dark green coach, its door bearing her brother-in-law's family coat of arms—a victorious golden griffin brandishing an arrow in its eagle's talons, its fallen pray beneath its lion's paw—but in no frame of mind to greet her sister's husband, she stepped back out of sight.

On the instant, the front door was thrown open and a blur of titian curls and green silk skirts sped to the carriage. "Orville!" his ecstatic wife cried before her lord had set more than one well-polished boot outside the chaise. "Is it truly you, my darling?"

"What is this?" Lord Townsend asked, a teasing light in his dark eyes. "I leave you for only a few days, my Bella, and I return to find you acting the butler. Is there no one employed in this establishment to open doors for my lady wife?"

"Bother the door!" his wife exclaimed inelegantly, casting herself upon her husband's neck. Tears spilled from her lovely hazel eyes. "Orville, my love, I have missed you so."

"That is as it should be," Lord Townsend replied, a not unpleased expression in evidence upon his handsome face. After giving his wife a quick buss, he disentangled himself from her arms and tried what he could to repair the damage done to his intricately tied neck cloth. "But let us not stand about entertaining the servants, my dear. May we not go inside? I swear I am in need of a bottle of something to remove the dust of the road from my throat, and if I remember correctly, your father's cellar boasts a not too contemptible Madeira, which—"

"Where have you been?" Bella asked, her joy at being reunited with her husband giving way to anger.

"Did I not tell you?"

Bristling, Bella replied, "You know you did not."

"Sorry, old girl. Must have slipped my mind. I went to call upon my cousin Archie. And a deuced time I had of it, I can tell you. Decent chap, and all that, but my cousin is grown dull as ditch water, not to mention filling his house with demmed cits. I don't mind telling you, my dear, it galls a fellow to be obliged to eat his mutton with a pack of—"

"Archie who?" Bella dug her heels in and would not let herself be led into the house. "You never mentioned a cousin, dull or otherwise."

Lord Townsend lowered his voice. "Don't talk about him much in the family; not that Archie cares a rap what the rest of us think. Married a mill owner's daughter, don't you know. Made him quite plump in the pockets. Got a passel of brats now, all of them with his long face. Regrettable, that."

As if recalling something he had almost forgotten, Lord Townsend added, "Oh, by the by, my dear, I promised Archie you would show his oldest gel about town next year."

Arabella gasped.

"The chit's only sixteen at the moment, of course, but my cousin wants her to have a come-out of sorts before she turns eighteen."

"You promised that *I* would sponsor a mill owner's grandchild? And one with a horse face? Townsend, how could you?"

"By Jove, the least we can do. Especially since Archie has agreed to see to that business of the fifteen thousand pounds."

"What!"

"Told you I would come about, old girl. I always do."

Bella's face was radiant. "Orville! How . . . how absolutely splendid. Does this mean we can go back home? Back to London?"

"Of course, my dear. The very reason I came by, to fetch my beautiful bride. Missed you, don't you know."

When Bella threw her arms around her husband's neck a second time, Madeline decided she could not witness any more of their reunion without succumbing to an attack of nausea. Furthermore, since Bella possessed the audacity to suggest killing the fatted calf in celebration of her prodigal husband's return, Madeline determined to get as far away from the house as possible. Considering all she had been through due to Lord Townsend's irresponsibility, Madeline was apt to suggest sparing the calf and killing her brother-in-law instead.

As always, the only sanctuary available, the only place where privacy was assured was the little bower near the brook. Aside from her desire to experience the calming affect of that secluded haven that never failed to refresh her soul, Madeline needed a quiet place to think and come to terms with her future. A future she now realized would never include a family and a home of her own. Nor would it include Philip.

It could not. Never again. Being with him—being his friend—would be too painful for her.

She would spend the rest of her life alone. Without love, without passion, and without the man who had taught her both those emotions. Without Philip. Because of Philip, Madeline had learned what it was like to love with all her heart and all her soul. And now no lesser love would do. There would never be another man for her. Far better to live a solitary existence than to accept someone who would always be second best.

Putting these thoughts aside for the moment, she hurried over the carpet of bluebells and through the woods, soon arriving at the stepping-stones that gave access to the Balenger side of the brook. With a dexterity born of practice, she tiptoed across. However, she did not go directly to the bower, choosing instead to pause on the sloping bank where just a week ago she had spied the little yellow primrose.

Madeline had been enchanted by the sight of the delicate blossom perched at the water's edge, valiantly living its life long after spring had passed it by. She had felt in sympathy with the unpretentious flower, and wanted to see it again, to see how it faired.

It was no longer there. No sign of it remained.

"It is gone," she whispered, experiencing a disproportionate sadness at its loss.

Not wanting to remain where the primrose had once thrived, Madeline would have moved away had she not become aware of another presence quite close by. Exactly as it had occurred a week ago, a man stood at the top of the bank. Only this time he did not speak. Nor did she spin about, as she had before, pitching helplessly into the water, for she knew the identity of the man who stood behind her.

Even without turning to look at him, she knew. Let a hundred years go by—a million—and she would still know.

With her gaze trained on the clear blue of the gently flowing water, she said, "You are recovered?"

Philip had approached the spot cautiously, sensing somehow that Madeline was there at the water's edge. Remembering how he had frightened her before, causing her to fall into the brook, he had remained quiet, waiting for her to turn and look at him. But she did not turn. And when she spoke, he knew she had felt his presence as surely as he had sensed hers.

"Recovered?" he repeated quietly.

No. He had not recovered. Not by any means. Not if she referred to the attack upon his soul.

Philip still reeled from the assault she had waged day after day with her warm smile, her gentleness, her honesty. And as if those weapons were not sufficient to render him a hapless victim, she had bombarded him with her bravery in the face of staggering danger.

Nor had she relented when he was shot, choosing instead to remain by his side, to chance her fate with his, wounding him with the one thing he had searched for his entire life—loyalty.

Then, when he was almost completely defeated, with only scant hope of escaping with his heart intact, she had inflicted the telling blow. She had kissed him.

Capitulating, he had kissed her in return. When his lovely mermaid had responded to his knees with such sweetness, such abandon, it had aroused in him a fierce longing for her—a longing he knew would require score upon score of years to assuage.

"No," he said softly, "I am not recovered."

Madeline turned quickly at his words, fear clutching at her heart, causing it to miss a beat. But even though his left arm rested in a sling, with the sleeve of his bottle green coat hanging empty, she knew he was well. He stood straight and tall, with his booted feet spread wide apart, like the buccaneer she would always think him, and his sun-bronzed face fairly glowed with health. In addition, there was a spark in his gray eyes, a light she had never seen there before.

As she watched, he descended the bank, striding toward her with a deliberateness, a purpose. He was coming to touch her. She knew that with a certainty. And as he drew nearer, and she felt the force of his personality and the strength of his powerful physique, she knew with equal certainty that she would not deny him that touch.

Stopping mere inches from her, he gazed into her eyes, his warm, tender scrutiny asking a question Madeline dared not trust herself to interpret, and as he continued to look at her, her knees threatened to give way beneath her. She reached out her hand to him for support, and as if she had moved at his request, he caught her hand and slowly lifted it to his mouth, pressing her palm to his firm, tantalizing lips. His warm breath caressed her skin, turning it into a living, yearning entity.

"I want you," he said, his voice a husky whisper.

When the tip of his tongue touched the sensitive flesh of her wrist, liquid fire scorched its way up her arm only to shatter into a thousand tributaries that, in turn, flowed throughout her body, heating it until she felt aflame. Madeline's breathing seemed to stop.

She tried to pull her palm away, but Philip did not let her retreat completely. Instead he placed her trembling hand upon his muscular chest, near his heart. His gaze never leaving hers, he slipped his arm around her waist and slowly, gently drew her close. She felt his heartbeat accelerate beneath her fingers, throbbing, throbbing, its tempo a perfect match to her own.

Just before his lips descended, claiming hers, he whispered, "I want you to marry me."

Lost in the magic of his kiss, it was several moments before Madeline realized the words had actually come from Philip, and were not part of some fantasy conversation going on inside her head.

Placing both hands on his chest, she pushed away from him as far as he would allow. "What did you say?" she asked, her voice hesitant, unsure.

"Will you sail away with me, my enchantress? To a place where dreams come true?"

Madeline shook her head, as if to free her mind of the trance his kisses had created. The delicious fog refused to be dispelled. "That is not what you said before."

Philip raised one eyebrow as if in question. "Are you telling me you will not sail away with me?"

"I—"

"I had hoped to take you to Greece," he whispered, coaxing her unresisting body close to his once again. When she surrendered and rested against him, his lips touched her forehead, moving softly as he spoke. "I know of a sun-kissed isle where the water is soft and warm upon a person's skin."

Mesmerized by the gentle movement of his lips, Madeline closed her eyes, enjoying his touch.

"I want to watch you frolic in the waves," he continued, "like the mermaid you are. Then, when you have swum to your heart's content, I want you to come to me, all warm and damp from the sea, and love me to my heart's content."

Quite bewitched by the picture he conjured of the two of them lying on a sunny beach, wrapped in one another's arms, Madeline was hard-pressed not to agree to his plan. "But I cannot go away with you," she said, the words painful in her throat. "Much as I would like to, I cannot."

His sad smile very nearly broke her heart. "Then, you will not marry me, my love? You will not let me take you to Greece for our wedding trip?"

She drew a deep, tremulous breath. "Are you teasing me, Philip? Oh, please. I could not bear it if I had misunderstood again."

The look of love in his eyes told her all she wanted to know, but she was reassured when he said the words.

"I love you, Madeline. I think I have loved you from the first moment I saw you. It is difficult to explain, and I do not understand it myself, but I feel almost as if some power beyond my control led me to you."

Tears of joy stung Madeline's eyes. "I know. It is the same for me. I feel as though I have loved you forever."

When he bent his head to kiss her, Madeline suddenly thought of all the reasons why theirs was an ineligible alliance. "But, Philip, I cannot. Surely you must realize that no one will believe I love you. All the old cats will think I married you for your money."

"Let them. I will know you did not. You accepted me as a laborer; now accept me as I truly am."

"And there is Lord Townsend," she said, honesty necessitating that she reveal all. "My brother-in-law will be forever pestering you to give him money."

"He is welcome to try. But you will recall that I have lived a number of years in hot climates. As a result, I am impervious to pests."

"And what of Arabella?"

"Lady Townsend is your sister. She will be welcome in our home whenever you choose to receive her. As for your other sister, I expect Priscilla to be much with us.

And when you take that saucy minx to town for her come-out, I want no expense spared. I will expect you both to make me proud."

Madeline's voice was choked with tears. "Philip, you are so good."

"Nothing of the sort," he assured her. "I wish only to make you happy."

"You do! I cannot tell you how happy. But you have not yet met my papa, and I must warn you about him. He is always behind with the world, and—"

Philip was obliged to brush a light kiss across her lips to hush her list of protests. "I mean to marry you, my love, if I have to play the pirate and steal you away. Now, will you stop all this nonsense and answer my question?"

Her heart bursting with joy, Madeline looked up into his eyes, discovering there a world filled with promise and excitement. "To be whisked away by a pirate," she said, "that would be quite something. If you only knew how I have longed for adventure."

"And you shall have it in abundance, my beautiful mermaid, for love is the greatest adventure of all. And I promise, I will love you forever."

"Oh, Philip."

Despairing of ever receiving the answer he sought, the buccaneer chose to accept that response as an affirmative reply. Exultant, he freed his injured arm from its sling so that he could hold his beloved as he had longed to do. "My beautiful mermaid," he whispered as he crushed her close to his chest, covering her mouth with his own, "let the adventure begin."